TALKING TO
ALASKA

Alaska

A NOVEL BY
ANNA WOLTZ

Translated by Laura Watkinson

A Rock the Boat Book

First published by Rock the Boat, an imprint of Oneworld Publications, 2021
Originally published in Dutch as *Alaska* by Em. Querido Kinderboeken Uitgeverij, 2016

Hardback 978-1-78607-880-3
Paperback 978-086154-096-9
eISBN 978-1-78607-968-8

This publication has been made possible with financial support
from the Dutch Foundation for Literature.

This book has been published with the support of Arts Council England and BookTrust.

Typeset by Divaddict Publishing Solutions Ltd
Printed and bound in Great Britain by Clays Ltd, Elcograf S.p.A.

Oneworld Publications
10 Bloomsbury Street,
London, WC1B 3SR, England

Stay up to date with the latest books,
special offers, and exclusive content from
Rock the Boat with our newsletter

Sign up on our website
oneworld-publications.com/rtb

For Fabeltje

SVEN

So this is the plan for today: to pull off such a brilliant stunt within the first five hours that the whole school instantly finds out who I am. They need to know me—before they hear about me.

I have no idea how I'm going to do it. I don't want to get thrown out of school on Day One, of course. But it's got to be big.

If I don't act soon, then within a week I'll be *that loser from 1B*. The kid who gets brought to school every day by his dad and picked up by his mom. Who's never allowed to be alone. The guy with the watch that beeps every couple of hours because it's time for some more pills.

I am not going to let that happen.

PARKER

My bike whizzes along the streets, because all the traffic lights are green today. It's as if the world wants to say to me: *Hey, look! I'm not really that bad.*

I'm in 1B this year, with twenty-seven other kids, and I've already met almost everyone. One boy was sick on the getting-to-know-you afternoon in June. Weird—he doesn't know a single other person in the class yet. I'm glad I can't remember what being born was like. Lying there, completely naked, in a world full of strangers. Faces you don't know, hands you don't know, nostril hairs you don't know. Maybe that's why babies scream so much.

Down one more long street, and then I'll be there. My breath's racing too, and my black dress is flapping in the wind. As I cycle past a man with a dog, I close my eyes for a moment. Less than a second, but it's long enough to picture Alaska.

I've been missing her for four months now, so during the daytime it feels almost normal for her not to be there. I'm used to the dog-shaped hole at home. I know I don't need to be careful with the door anymore, and all the blankets covered in white hairs went into the washing machine ages ago.

But at night I dream about her. Sometimes she's been hurt, and I run along dark streets to a brightly lit animal hospital that's eighty-seven stories high. And sometimes— and this is way worse—she's just there. She's lying beside me on the sofa and I'm stroking the soft bristles on her nose. Calmly, quietly, because I know we'll sit there together a thousand more times.

And then I wake up and feel empty.

I'm not going to pay any attention to the Tips for First Years on the internet. I'm planning to skip puberty. Why would I want to "pimp" my backpack with glittery flowers? And who exactly gets to decide that lunchboxes are dumb, and sandwich bags are cool? Those websites give you all these long lists full of tips, and then right at the end they always go and say: *But whatever you do, always be yourself.*

Well, it's not like I was going to pretend to be a leopard, is it? Or a hot-air balloon? Nope, of course not. But, *be yourself*? Is that what they tell the bullies and the liars and the people who are cruel to animals too? And all the people who are in prison and everyone who hasn't been caught yet?

Hey, bad guys! Don't forget the most important thing of all: just be yourself!

If I ever have to give anyone some tips, I'll say: *You know, maybe you just happen to be a massive idiot. Or a coward. And in that case, you're better off being someone else.*

SVEN

My dad dropped me off at the gates. I wanted him to stop one street sooner, but he refused.

It's hot for September. I'm not wearing a coat, so everyone can see the blue strap around my wrist. It's supposed to look like some kind of cool wristband, but I still feel like an animal. A lost pet wandering around with its owner's telephone number.

As I walk toward the school, I deliberately don't think about my friends who are still on vacation. On the other side of the country they don't go back to school until next week. They'll be in the second year. But I'm starting all over again, back in the first year.

I head inside, pretending to be normal.

The floors are black and white. The lockers are green and yellow. Nine hundred students all together—that's a herd. A screaming mob with bags that bang into everything, fists that shove, zits about to pop, phones that vibrate as soon as they pick up the school Wi-Fi.

I'm not scared.

I'm never scared.

But when I see the stairs, three stories of rock-hard concrete steps, I stand still for a moment.

When my mom started going on about the stairs to the principal, I could have killed her. And last week, when I got that email with all the rules for my special key for the elevator, I spent the rest of the day slamming doors.

But here's the worst thing. Now that I'm standing here—surrounded by all that bare concrete and all those floors—I'm glad.

I'm thirteen, not eighty. But I'm glad that I've got a special key for the elevator.

A deafening bell rings throughout the building. It sounds as if the universe is on fire.

Now you can really tell who's new. The First Years all jump and start trotting. The rest don't speed up one bit.

So I've got the elevator key. But where's the elevator?

PARKER

We're sitting in complete silence, looking at the French teacher, but I know everyone else is fizzing and popping inside too, just like me. Maybe that girl at the front, the one with the black curls, will be my best friend. Maybe I'll like that boy with the freckles.

Everyone in my old class has gone to other schools. No one here knows me, and no one knows what happened this summer. This is a new beginning, I tell myself. Maybe it's not just the traffic lights this morning that are turning green for me. Maybe the world really isn't that bad after all.

"*Bienvenue!*" shouts Mr. Gomes. He's wearing a checked shirt with short sleeves. A dragon tattoo coils around his forearm. "*J'espère que vous avez tous passé de bonnes vacances.*"

I don't dare to move. Am I the only one who can't understand a word he's saying? Did we have homework for today? Already?

And then the classroom door swings open.

Standing in the doorway is a boy with messy blond hair and faded jeans. I know who it is right away: it's him. The twenty-eighth member of 1B—the one who was sick on the getting-to-know-you day. As quickly as possible, I try to take everything in: blue eyes, medium build, gray T-shirt, Band-Aid on his chin, a bit taller than me, dirty sneakers.

"*Alors!*" shouts Mr. Gomes. "*Vous êtes en retard. Que s'est-il passé?*"

"Um," says the boy in the doorway. He gives the teacher a puzzled look. "*Une baguette, s'il vous-plaît?*"

It feels like we're Coke bottles that have been shaken about for hours. And now the blond boy has unscrewed all twenty-seven of our plastic tops at once. All of us burst out laughing at the very same moment. In my ancient vacation scrapbook, I wrote in a seven-year-old's scrawl: *you say OON BAGET SEEVOOPLAY.* They were the very first French words I ever learned. I was amazed when the fat French baker actually went and fetched a stick of bread for me.

We go on laughing and laughing—and suddenly we aren't a bunch of assorted kids anymore. We're a class.

"Sorry..." The boy in the doorway shrugs. "I got a D for French last year. I'm Sven."

Mr. Gomes picks up a piece of paper from his desk. His eyes fly over the words. "Sven Beekman?"

The boy nods.

"Aha," says Gomes. "Right..." There's a cautious sound to his voice. "OK, Sven, go and sit down."

And then he looks at us and his talking-to-eggshells voice has gone. "Listen up, 1B! How can you learn French when you've just been dropped into a class full of new people? That's right: you can't. So we're going to get to know one another first."

We all have to write down three funny things about ourselves. Two things that are true. And one lie.

"*Par exemple...*" says Gomes. "That means 'for example'. I'll tell you some things about me. One: I love eating fried grasshoppers. Two: I live in a tree house. And three: I played soccer for Ajax juniors."

The boys in the back row start yelling out which story must be the lie, but he shakes his head.

"I'm the only one who doesn't have to tell you today which one's made up. You've got a whole school year to find out. And now—get to work. Make your own lists."

As, all around me, pens click and notebooks open for the very first time, I stare at the gigantic black-and-white photograph on the wall: the Eiffel Tower in the rain. I search my brain for funny things to say, but instead I just see videos that I most definitely do not want to watch. They're for viewers over the age of sixteen—at least!—but they've been playing inside my head for weeks now.

That's how it works. They put scary labels on made-up things like films and games: *Warning! Violence! Swear words! Sex! May cause fear and anxiety!*

But when something actually happens, in real life, there's no sign of any warning labels. Criminals do not respect parental guidelines.

Five minutes later, there are big black lines scribbled all over the first page of my book, but there are also three sentences.

When it's your turn, you have to say your name first. Some of the others have come up with stuff that just makes me think: *Wow. If that's the weirdest thing you can imagine, you must have a very nice life.*

My favorite color is blue.

I play hockey.

I went to Spain this summer.

And then it's my turn. I take a deep breath. "I'm Parker."

It's the first thing I've said since breakfast with my brothers.

"I'm called Parker because I was born in a park. Two years ago, we secretly scattered my grandma's ashes at Efteling. And I can bark 'Jingle Bells'."

It's a few seconds before anyone makes a sound. And then the Coke bottles explode again. Everyone starts yelling all at once. Saying that scattering ashes at amusement parks isn't allowed. And that Parker isn't a girl's name. And asking if we emptied the urn in the Fairytale Forest or on one of the rides.

"You can bark 'Jingle Bells'?" Sven yells above everyone else. He's looking at me. His eyes are as blue as a Siberian husky's.

I nod.

"Go on, then!" he shouts.

He hasn't had his turn yet, so I don't know anything about him. No things that are true. No things that are lies.

I look at my book and think about Alaska.

Last Christmas, when she was still a puppy, the two of us must have watched the YouTube video of the dogs singing "Jingle Bells" a hundred times. The first time, she just sat on my lap, perfectly still. Her claws digging into my thigh, her puppy nose cocked at an angle, her eyes as round as marbles. Amazed to discover that such a thing existed: fellow dogs who could sing. By the sixteenth time, we were barking along with the dog choir. And after fifty times, Alaska was standing up on her pudgy little puppy legs and yapping away at the silent computer, because she thought it was time for another concert.

"You're too chicken!" shouts Sven.

I look back at him without blinking. There are a thousand things I'm too chicken to do. But this isn't one of them.

I lift my chin, because that's what Alaska and I always did. And then I begin.

SVEN

Seriously. The people in this town are even crazier than I thought. In the very first class, this girl actually starts *barking*.

Her name is Parker Montijn. She's thin and pale, like she's just back from a trip to the North Pole. She's the only girl in the class who wears black and the only girl who doesn't smile.

She puts her pointed nose in the air and barks away so realistically that you want to make an emergency call to the animal-protection people. It's like she's just swallowed a dog. A live one.

But halfway through the song she stops.

She looks around and I see her cheeks go bright red. Whoa, I thought she was doing it on purpose. That this was *her* brilliant stunt. But she's only just realized how dumb she looks. And that the rest of the class can't stop laughing.

"Do 'Frosty the Snowman'!" shouts Ben.

"Or 'Rudolph the Red-Nosed Reindeer'," yells Sol. "I bet a dog can do that one!"

That's it. She's had it.

From today until the day she dies, Parker Montijn will be the girl who stirred a dog into her corn flakes for breakfast and started barking in the first class.

At lunchtime, Sol and Ben ask me to play soccer with them, but I just shake my head.

I tell them I'm a competitive swimmer. That I don't go running around in a herd, chasing after a ball. But secretly I'm completely exhausted, even though it's only midday.

Stupid pills.

Slowly, I walk down the hallway, chewing a spelt-bread sandwich with avocado.

Since we moved here, my mom hasn't had a job. Now she just does two things: worries about me and bakes bread. Sourdough with linseed. Date bread with goji berries and chia seeds.

But no matter what superfoods she uses, I'm still me.

Parker the dog girl is standing in the middle of the entrance hall. All alone.

Black dress, white legs. She matches the checked tiles. With a serious look on her face, she's studying every window and every door and counting something on her fingers.

As I walk past her, I quietly hum "Jingle Bells." But I stop when I see her face.

"Think it's funny, do you?" she asks fiercely.

She's looking right at me. Her eyes are pale gray with a dark line around the iris. "It was your fault I started singing!"

"Is that what you call it here?" I ask. "Frogs croak, sheep bleat—and dogs sing?"

"You challenged me!"

I put my hands in my pockets.

"When I was nine," I say, "I jumped into the canal in the middle of winter. My mom asked me later why I'd done it, and I told her someone had challenged me. She said it was a really stupid reason for nearly drowning."

"She was right," says Parker.

She looks all around the black-and-white-checked entrance hall.

"I've got stuff to do," she says.

Without glancing back at me, she walks away.

A little later, when I'm alone in the hall, I clench my fists. This is my chance.

Everyone else is sitting outside in the sunshine, and I'm in here. It's time for my brilliant stunt, for the whole school to find out who I am.

What should I do? Set off the fire alarm? Call the police about a suspicious package? Climb on to the roof?

But then I pause.

I thought each and every one of my brain cells was working to come up with a stunt. But suddenly I notice how quiet it is here. How empty the halls are. And that I'm all alone.

Can I remember the last time I was without one single other person? Without a camera, without an alarm button, without a dog?

No.

I should be over the moon—free at last! I've finally managed to escape from all that insanely annoying worrying and fussing. All the rules that make it impossible to live.

But I'm not happy at all.

I can feel cold sparks at the back of my neck, and God knows what's happening inside my head right now. Suddenly I couldn't care less about pulling off any brilliant stunts—I just want one thing.

To get back to the mob. To stop being alone.

PARKER

The sixth class of the day is homeroom.

All the windows in the classroom are open. A wasp is flying high above our heads, and out in the school playground we can hear shouting voices that are already free.

Sven Beekman is the last to arrive again. I have no idea why he has to come late to every class. Ben's kept a seat for him, and Ziva, the girl with the black curls, smiles at him.

I act like he doesn't exist.

While everyone else is fiddling around with their notebooks and pens, I quickly check my cell phone. I've already sent my mom four messages and she answered within five minutes every time, just like we agreed. I secretly give the start screen a little stroke with my finger. It still has a photo of Alaska on it.

Our homeroom teacher is called Mr. Blockmans and, even if you count the skeleton in the biology room, he must be the oldest person in the entire school. A hundred years ago, he was a student here himself, and one of the first things he tells us is that the basement beneath the multimedia center is haunted. Some of the other kids giggle and shiver dramatically, but I just stare at the map on the wall.

"And now," says Blockmans, "I need to go through the school rules with you. About the use of so-called smartphones in particular. There's some…"

He stops.

In the otherwise silent classroom, someone is laughing.

Not in a normal way, but all weird and deep. It sounds kind of menacing. Like a ghost that's stuck in a loop.

"HA-HA-HA-HA-HA…"

I feel goosebumps on my arms as I turn to look. Along with the rest of the class.

The noise is coming from Sven's mouth. From his body— but he doesn't look like himself anymore. His eyes have rolled back into his head, and he's making these weird smacking noises with his lips now.

"What's wrong with him?" says Ziva.

"Hey, Sven…" Ben shakes Sven's arm, but there's no reaction.

Sven's mouth opens and closes. His eyes are staring. And that spooky noise is coming from his throat.

Sol takes out his phone. "I'm calling an ambulance!"

"There's no need," says Blockmans calmly. "Sol, put your phone away. Sven will be able to hear us again in a few seconds."

The girls have all clasped their hands over their mouths, and Sol is still clutching his phone. The screen's lit up—he's already keyed in the emergency number.

I don't do anything. Those videos I don't want to see keep flashing through my head. They always start playing when things get scary.

And then the weird laughter suddenly stops. Sven blinks, picks up his pen and looks down at his book, as if there's nothing wrong. As if he has no idea he was just possessed by a ghost. Holding our breath, we all stare at him. His pen hovers over the paper, ready to get to work. But Blockmans hasn't given us anything to do yet.

After a couple of seconds, Sven looks up. And then he sees us staring.

SVEN

It feels like I'm surfacing from underwater.

It's happened again. It must have.

I put down my pen and wipe the drool from my chin. They're staring at me.

So this is it. From now on, I'm going to be *that loser from 1B.*

"You were gone for just a little while," says Blockmans in his deep voice. "Half a minute maybe, that's all. You were smacking your lips and laughing."

I look at the chair in front of me. Inside my head, I'm yelling all the swear words I know.

*　　*　　*

Blockmans came to visit me at home twice this summer. The second time, when we were sitting under the big yellow umbrella in the yard, I was out of it for a little while too. And he must have remembered what my mom did next: she told me how long it had lasted and exactly what I'd done.

"Are you OK?" asks Blockmans. "Would you like something to drink or..."

I shake my head.

After a fit, the world is a little fluid. It takes a while for the lines to become solid again. For my brain to remember how to store everything: sounds go with sounds, colors go with colors. Words go with words.

I clear my throat.

"I feel fine," I say too loudly. "But I think Ziva and Elin could do with some water."

I was out of it, but they saw it happen.

And now, on Day One, they already know more about me than I do.

As the girls take gulps of water and rub each other's backs, I clench my teeth. Right now I could beat up the entire school.

Or maybe not. I'm so exhausted. I just want to go to bed.

Blockmans looks at me. "Would you like to explain it to them yourself?"

I nod. If I start acting sorry for myself now, I'll just be the epileptic kid for the rest of the year. I stare at a wasp that doesn't understand how the open window works. It keeps smashing into the glass.

And then I tell them. That I have epilepsy.

I really, really hate that word. If there was a sport called epilepsy, there's no way in a million years I'd ever choose to join the club.

But this isn't something you choose.

It started a year ago. Just like that, out of nowhere. I had a short circuit in my head. My brain cells were firing off too many signals. Like when you bash away at all the keys on a computer at the same time, and the whole thing stops working. Well, every time my brain fires off too many sparks, I stop working too.

"When I'm having a fit," I say, without looking at anyone, "I'm completely out of it. I could break my arm or fall into a fire without realizing. And I can't tell what's broken until it's over. Like now, when I saw you all staring at me. Yeah, well, that's when I know it's happened."

They're still staring, but I don't want to see. I know those expressions. When their mom or dad asks them later, "How was your first day?", they won't tell them about French and math. They'll tell them about me. But not really about me— just about my messed-up brain.

"That one was a small seizure. But sometimes I have a big one and everything goes haywire. I don't feel them coming. I just fall over. And my whole body starts shaking. Usually it stops by itself, but if it's still going on after five minutes and my face turns blue, then it's a good idea to call an ambulance."

While I'm talking, all I can think is: *I DON'T WANT THIS.*

I didn't want to join the epilepsy club. But I've still been in an ambulance seventeen times in the past year. I had to give up swimming and I'm not allowed to ride my bike anymore. I sleep downstairs in our new house, and I have my own bathroom, so that I never have to climb stairs.

I hate our new house.

"All the teachers," says Blockmans, "know about Sven's condition and about when they need to call an ambulance. And Sven and his parents have written a letter for you. With extra information."

He picks up a stack of paper from his desk and starts handing out copies. This is the lamest class presentation ever.

If I have as many seizures this year as I did last year, I'll have to retake the year again. I'll end up being the only sixty-year-old student in the school—and I'll still be getting Ds for French.

"It's not contagious," I say loudly. "And when I'm not having a seizure, there's nothing wrong with me. Nothing at all."

I can tell from their faces that they don't believe me.

Hey, I don't even believe it myself.

In two seconds' time, I could be lying on the floor, twitching away. Wherever I go, whatever I do, there's always that voice inside my head: *It could happen at any moment. If it's not this second, it'll be the next one. Or the one after that.*

PARKER

A policeman once told me that being observant is something you can learn. And he also said that if you start paying attention only after something's happened, then it's already too late.

So, by the end of the first day, I've noted everything about everyone in 1B. Their first names, their surnames. I could give twenty-seven accurate descriptions. And I know where all the fire hoses and the emergency exits are.

In the hall on my way out, I try to make myself as small as possible. The girls around me can't stop talking about Sven Beekman. They already thought he was funny and kind of cool, but now they can feel sorry for him too. Like one of those action heroes in a movie who suddenly reveals that he grew up in an orphanage. And that he silently cried himself to sleep every night—which makes you like him even more. Even if he does kill loads of people.

Well, that's not how it works with me.

I hold on tightly to my phone as I walk through the entrance hall. Giants are yelling all around me, but if my phone starts vibrating, I'll feel it right away. I look out through the window—and then I stop so suddenly that I cause a multiple collision.

But I don't feel the impact at all.

Inside my head, I hear a frantic yelp of exploding happiness. The way dogs howl when they haven't seen you for a whole week. I can hardly believe it and yet I'm absolutely certain: out there in the sunshine, sitting on the gray slabs beside the bike shed… It's Alaska!

I haven't seen her for four months, but I still remember every little hair. Every fold in her white-blond fur. She's sitting beside a woman I don't know, waiting in the school playground. She's not wearing an ordinary collar like the one she had when she was with us, but a harness and a bright-yellow vest. She's watching everyone really closely, and all I want to do is rush outside and hug her forever and ever.

But then the woman waves at someone who's coming out of the school. Alaska starts wagging her tail in excitement. The fringe of hair on her tail swishes, her dark eyes twinkle, her black mouth smiles.

I peer around. And then I see who she's wagging her tail for.

He doesn't even look at her. He hands his backpack to his mom and takes Alaska's leash, ignoring her sweeping tail. She pushes her nose into his hand, but he just walks off without saying anything to her.

I stand there at the window and think: *So this is what it feels like. A short circuit inside your head.*

For four months now, I've been trying to find out where she is. Who her new owners are. In my mind, I pictured her running in the woods through patches of sunlight and jumping into stinky ditches. But I never knew who put her in the bath afterward. Or whose leg she rested her head on when she wanted to play. And now I know.

Alaska belongs to Sven.

SVEN

I can't believe Mom's brought the beast to school. Right on the very first day.

Everyone's staring at that vest on her back, of course. Written in huge letters on the side, it says, *ASSISTANCE DOG. DO NOT PET*. But, as always, everyone wants to do just one thing: to stroke the hairy monster. Without speaking to the mob around me and without looking at my mom, I tug at the leash.

I've already messed things up with 1B by having that fit. And now the rest of the school has seen me with an assistance dog.

When people are in wheelchairs or when they're blind, everyone just gets it. But with me, everyone thinks: *Huh? An assistance dog? But why? He doesn't look like he needs any assistance! So what's the story?*

I never used to feel like thumping strangers in the street and giving them black eyes. But now I want to do it on an almost daily basis.

*   *   *

The sidewalk, the cars, the houses—the sun has made everything boiling hot. I can feel sweat on my forehead and I pretend not to hear my mom's hundred thousand questions.

I don't get it. Every assistance dog has to do a course, but parents don't have to learn anything.

The harness has a blue square on it, with a big white letter L. That's because the beast is still in training. Well, they should stick an L on my mom too. And as far as I'm concerned, they should never take it off.

I storm past houses and parked bikes and a café full of people with ice creams. But just as I'm about to cross the road, I have to stop.

The beast has sat down.

I swear at her.

She's sitting on her bum and refusing to move. The leash is tight. I pull, but she doesn't budge, not even an inch. Her dark eyes look guiltily at me. As if she'd really love to come with me—but sorry, it's impossible.

"Oh, come on!" I yell. "Stop being so difficult!"

And then I feel my mom's hand around my wrist. She pulls me back so that the leash is not so tight, and she takes a doggy treat out of her pocket.

"Good dog," she says quietly to the beast. "Well done!"

*　　*　　*

I can tell from her hand on my wrist how angry she is. I can't hear it in her voice though.

"I'm well aware," she says to me, just as quietly, "that you'd imagined your first day at your new school a bit differently. But whatever the problem is, it's not Alaska's fault. She's here to help you. And chances are she'll save your life one day."

She lets go of my wrist.

"You can yell at me as much as you like. But not at Alaska. And if you don't take her training seriously, then I'll call Yvonne and tell her it's not working out. And that she should find another child for Alaska, someone who really will do their best for her."

I know all of that. And honestly, yelling at the dog feels way worse than yelling at my mom.

But Mom's always been around. And the beast only came along when I got sick. I look at the dog and it seems as if not only her vest but every inch of her white fur is covered in words: *YOU HAVE EPILEPSY. YOU ARE NOT NORMAL. WITHOUT ME YOU WILL DIE.*

I go and stand on her right. Sigh deeply. And look at her.

"Alaska, let's go!" I say, in that awful tone of voice that kindergarten teachers use.

And yes, that doggy bum finally comes up off the sidewalk. Looking relieved, the beast trots across the street with me.

So that's how to do it. That's what Yvonne taught us, and that's what we have to practice every day. At every curb, I say,

"Alaska, sit"—and she sits. And then I say, "Alaska, let's go"—and we cross the street together.

Without a command, she refuses to move. Because in her doggy universe there are no angry owners who are in a foul mood. In her universe there are only owners who have seizures. And that makes it all very simple.

Cross the street with a command: life.

Cross the street without a command: death.

And she's right too. That's the worst thing about it. Before I had her, I once walked out into the street when I was having a seizure, and I got hit by a car. Didn't quite die. But nearly.

PARKER

Now I know exactly what I need to do. I'm going to kidnap Alaska.

My feet pedal as fast as they can; the sun beats down on my head. I should be scared, because my mom's in the store, and closing time is getting nearer and nearer. My shadow of a dad has picked up my little brothers from school for the first time, and the streets are full of people, all wanting to *be themselves*.

But I'm not scared today. I'm angry. For the past four months, whenever I was missing Alaska, I could at least think: *She's an assistance dog now. She's making life easier for someone who needs her help.* It felt a bit like giving your favorite cuddly toy to a homeless kid. Or donating your pocket money to people who have just survived a hurricane.

But now I know the truth. Never in a million years would I give a single cent or even my most pathetic cuddly toy to Sven Beekman. But he's got Alaska. He didn't even stroke her when she was standing there waiting for him and wagging her tail. He doesn't deserve her.

I pedal so hard that the world becomes a blur. People fly past and I can't remember any details. If something bad happens now, I'll be a terrible witness, that's for sure.

Tonight I'm going to Sven's house, because Alaska can't stay there, not even for one more day. Just imagine living with someone who suddenly rolls his eyes back into his head and starts laughing all spookily. Or who lies on the ground twitching until he's so blue in the face that you have to call an ambulance.

And what if you're not a human, but a dog? Then you'd have no idea why you had to start wearing a weird yellow vest. And stacks of handouts about epilepsy wouldn't be any help at all.

The front door's closed, but I can already hear my little brothers yelling. I drop my bag in the hall and run into the living room.

Dad's sitting silently at the computer. There's a puddle of lemonade on the table with a scattering of swollen corn flakes in it, and the floor looks like a plague of locusts just passed through. My little brothers have only been home for half an hour.

"Parker!" yells Dex.

"Where were you?" screams Finn.

"Soldiers, MARCH!" shouts Joey.

Dex is nine, Finn is seven, Joey is six. My mom and dad say it was deliberate. That they had four children on purpose—and I believe them. Of course, they weren't planning on three lots of ADHD. But hey. There were other things they weren't planning on too.

I walk over to my dad and put my arms around his neck.

He clears his throat. "How was school?" His eyes are still looking at the screen, but his hand gives my arm a quick squeeze.

"You know," I say. "OK."

I don't tell him about "Jingle Bells." Or about Sven's spooky fit. Or about Alaska either.

"Have you guys got homework to do?" I ask, as I wipe up the drowned corn flakes.

"No!" shout my little brothers. "Course not. It was the first day back!"

They grab their Super Soakers and start marching around the table, shouting military commands. I see Dad wince, and I'd really love to take their stupid water pistols into the backyard and burn them. But all the other boys in the street have got them. And my brothers are nine and seven and six. They can't help it that the parental guidelines are all wrong.

My dad is thirty-nine. So, according to those stupid warnings, he's old enough to handle any film in the world. But that's not true.

"Soldiers!" I yell above the noise. "We are going on an expedition to locate provisions!"

Dex, Finn and Joey beam at me. When I suddenly found myself without a dog, for a while I tried to teach my brothers how to fetch and how to walk nicely on the leash. It was a disaster, until I discovered that they didn't want to be dogs. They wanted to be soldiers.

Our street smells of freshly watered grass and hot tarmac. Dex takes the leash, with Finn in the middle and Joey bringing up the rear. Their brown hair is always in a mess, they

32

have corn flakes stuck to their chins, and their clothes are never clean for more than ten minutes.

"Left, RIGHT, left, RIGHT!" I shout so loud that the lime trees rustle. The more fiercely I yell and the sterner I sound, the more my brothers like it.

I hate marching and uniforms and shooting with water pistols. It gives me the shivers, and I think it should be banned. But I also hate going into stores by myself. So now I have my own private army. I send them out on exploratory expeditions for chocolate sprinkles and pickled gherkins. They lug the heavy shopping bags around, because that's all part of the military campaign.

And they're here. They protect me. At least that's what they tell me.

SVEN

When I wake up, the sun's already low in the sky. I'm thirteen, but after a day at school I need a two-hour nap.

I stay lying there, because I don't want to go into the living room. Sometimes I don't know what's worse: being sick, or the way my mom and dad look at me now.

There's an iron wall inside my head.

I just don't think about it. How things will turn out, I mean. If we can't find any medication that works.

Like, with driving a car. And girls. And a normal job.

And if I can't ever swim in a competition again, if all I can do is *look* at the sea.

No. I don't want to think about these things.

My hand pats the quilt beside me. As if it's not my hand, but someone else's.

The beast jumps up on the bed next to me. She lies so close that not even a flea could squeeze in between us. I can hear her tail on the quilt: *thud, thud, thud.*

It's far too warm for a doggy hot-water bottle, but I let her stay there. I stroke her head and her floppy triangular ears. Most golden retrievers are yellow or brown, but this is a dog made of snow. Her eyes, mouth, and nose stand out pitch black against the white.

At home she doesn't have to wear that dumb vest. At home I can sometimes forget for a while that she's an assistance dog. And then she just seems like the dog I've been begging for—ever since I could talk.

PARKER

At two o'clock in the morning, I awake with a start. For a moment I think someone's broken in and that I can hear our alarm going off and that men with knives are wandering around downstairs. But then I remember what's going on.

I'm going to kidnap Alaska.

I take out my cell phone from under the pillow and quickly swipe the alarm clock off. My eyes are still half shut, and it feels like I've only been asleep for ten minutes. But if I don't go now, I'll have to wait another two days. My mom and dad are on rations: they're allowed to take a sleeping pill one night, but not the next. And so on.

On the nights without sleeping pills, they're constantly prowling around the house. On the nights *with* sleeping pills, they're dead to the world for six hours.

Just putting on my black pants and a dark-green polo neck, I'm already hyperventilating. I've stolen my dad's woolly hat from the box of winter clothes. If I pull it all the way down over my head, it comes past my chin. Before I went to bed, I used the kitchen scissors to cut out holes for my eyes and mouth.

So now it's a balaclava. It's lying beside the frog nightlight on my desk and peering at me with its holes. I look back at it, feeling a bit sick. In my mind, I can see the pictures from the security camera again. A film for viewers over the age of forty. Without sound. But with violence.

With trembling fingers, I stuff the hat into my backpack. My bike keys are already in there, with a flashlight, a rope that I'm planning to use as a leash for Alaska, and a packet of dog biscuits that I've been keeping in my sock drawer for the past four months.

Downstairs, the new alarm is on. I can't get to the control panel without setting it off, so I climb out of my window. I've already done this a thousand times when I didn't need to— just because it's fun jumping on to the shed roof and then climbing down the trellis to the ground.

It's one of those nights that come along only a couple of times a year. The dark air is made of velvet. There's a faint smell of grilled meat in the air—the last of the barbecuers have only just gone inside. Now the entire town is asleep.

The only ones awake are the thieves.

Five weeks ago, I would have thought this was great. Silently unchaining my bike from the fence and riding off down the empty street. Without lights for the first two hundred yards, and then with. Knowing that I've memorized the route to Sven's house. Acting like it's normal to be cycling across town at quarter past two in the morning with my hair fluttering in the warm breeze.

But it's not five weeks ago—it's now.

My heart's thumping away; the palms of my hands are clammy. I try to focus on Alaska: the little pads on her feet, the way she always lay dreaming with her four legs in the air. If everything goes well, I'll be able to bury my face in her fur in half an hour.

But men in balaclavas keep flashing through my mind. I wish my marching brothers were here. My shadow of a dad. My mom who never cries.

Just when I'm so scared that I want to scream, I realize that I'm there.

A street full of new houses. There's still fresh sand between the paving stones—I can feel it under my wheels. I've studied the street on Google Maps. The yards back on to an enormous empty field. Maybe they're going to build houses on it too, but there's nothing there yet.

I pedal to the end of the row of houses and then get off and push my bike, sneaking around to the back of the houses. I'm panting as if I've just run a marathon. I still haven't put the balaclava on. Sven mustn't recognize me, but to anyone else I'll look way more suspicious with the balaclava on than without.

My eyes are already so used to the darkness that I don't need the flashlight. As I drag my bike across the sandy field, I count the backyards. Alaska lives at the seventh.

I thought I could use my bike to help climb over the fence, but Sven's yard turns out to have been specially designed for burglars. The gate's locked, of course, but the planks are arranged horizontally with gaps between them—it's like climbing up a ladder. And then back down again.

I stand there in his backyard, panting. A gleaming pond, white yard chairs, flowers that smell sweet in the night. All of the windows are dark. I pull the balaclava over my head and hate myself. But this is not about burglary. This is about Alaska.

My entire plan is based on one thing: the heat. The day was sweltering, and the night is muggy. Most people have no air conditioning—they just leave the windows open. And that's what I'm hoping for. That Sven's parents aren't like mine. That they don't have an alarm. And that they sleep with the windows open.

I sneak to the back door. I try the handle—but the door is closed. I don't know anyone who sleeps right behind the back door, so I shine my flashlight inside for three seconds. A deserted kitchen. No sleeping people. And no sleeping dog either.

On tiptoe, I make my way to the sliding glass doors to the left of the kitchen. It must be the living room. I touch the doors in the dark and then hold my breath. They're slightly open.

Quickly, I crouch down. Grab my flashlight. Hold on to the door with one hand. And then I feel something wet move across my fingers.

Just when I'm about to scream, a white muzzle pokes through the gap. I hear frantic whining. A warm tongue greedily licks my hand. As if nothing else in the world tastes as good as my fingers.

"Alaska!" I whisper to the nose. It sounds like a sigh, but it feels like a yell that goes all the way to the stars.

The whining is getting louder. I hear her tail swishing, her claws tapping on the floor. She's walking back and forth behind the door—any minute now she's going to start barking because all that happiness is too much for her to handle.

I pull as hard as I can at the sliding doors, but the gap doesn't get even the tiniest bit wider.

Any minute now *I'm* going to start barking because I can't handle all that happiness either. In a flash, I think back to this morning, when I looked like such a complete idiot in front of everyone in my new class, and when that horrible Sven hummed at me at lunchtime. But if I can kidnap Alaska, none of that will matter anymore.

I cautiously feel around the inside of the glass door. There's a handle halfway down. I give it a tug—it swings upward, and suddenly the door moves. I slip inside and close it behind me. If I let Alaska into the yard now, she'll start barking away and galloping around in circles.

I'm here.

It's pitch dark in the room, but that doesn't matter. You don't need light to hug.

I drop down on to my knees, wishing I had a thousand arms. Now I realize just how badly I've missed her. How completely. Not only with my head, but with my whole body—with my hands and ears and eyes and lips.

"Yes, yes, good girl!" I keep whispering. "Shush, Alaska. I'm happy too. Yes, I missed you too. Ssh, Alaska—quiet, girl!"

I unzip my backpack to take out the rope. And then a light goes on.

Alaska's tail is swishing air into my face, but I can't breathe. I just blink.

I thought I was in the living room, but this is a bedroom. Against the wall, six feet away, is a single bed with a lamp beside it. And in that bed is Sven.

SVEN

The ocean is rushing inside my head. My heart is thumping. I can't move.

There's a dark shadow next to my bed. With thin arms and a black head with three holes. The hole for the left eye is higher than the right eye. Its mouth is a triangle.

Alaska's acting like she's been waiting for this moment all her life. She's dancing around and whining like an idiot. Her tail's spinning like a propeller.

If I hadn't heard that whispering voice first, I'd be screaming the house down.

But it crept up on me. Like a hill getting steeper without you realizing.

First I dreamed someone was slipping into my room. And as I woke up, I heard that whispering voice. "Good girl, Alaska. I'm happy too. Yes, I missed you too, Alaska..."

And now I'm completely awake and my brain has finally

grasped that—yes, really, truly—SOMEONE IS IN MY
BEDROOM.

The shadow stands up and takes a step toward the sliding
doors.

"Wait!" I call. No idea why—my voice belongs to someone
else.

The shadow stops.

It's a girl, I can see that now. Suddenly I remember that I'm
only wearing boxers. And it's way too hot for a quilt.

Whoa, I must still be dreaming.

Being stared at in the middle of the night by a strange girl
while you're lying half naked in bed—it sounds like a dream,
right?

"Are you real?" I whisper. Dumbest question ever, but hey.

Her hands are the only parts of her that aren't covered.

"Yes," she whispers back, as her fingers become fists. "I'm
real."

I can't tell anything from her voice. Not her age, no unusual
accent. No turned-up nose, no beautiful eyes, no weird chin.

The only one who can remember how to move is Alaska.
She bounds over, puts her front paws on the bed, gives my
bare stomach a lick and runs back to the shadow.

If that beast weren't so ridiculously happy, I'd call the
police.

"You know her name's Alaska," I whisper. "How?"

I act like everything is under control. As if I have a girl in a balaclava standing by my bed every night.

"Well?"

Her fists vanish as soon as the beast comes anywhere near. She strokes that white head as if her hands are hungry.

"It was me who named her," she says so quietly that I can barely hear it. "Alaska belonged to me first."

I sit up. "That beast lived with you?"

She nods.

Of course I already knew that Alaska had other owners before. She was nearly a year old when she came to us. But I didn't need to know about it. I mean, if you get a second-hand wheelchair, or a pair of used crutches, then you don't need to know anything about the previous owner, do you?

"Take that balaclava off!"

I want to find out what she looks like, but she shakes her head.

"I've got an alarm button here," I say. "If I press it, my mom and dad will be in the room within three seconds."

"Why do you have an alarm button?" she whispers. "In case of burglars?"

"In case I have a seizure." I run my fingers through my hair, and I can feel that it's sticking straight up. "I have epilepsy. That's –"

"I know what it is," she snaps.

I was all ready to trot out my little lecture.

"Really? OK...Well, sometimes I have a seizure at night, and then the dog presses the alarm with her nose. And my mom and dad come rushing downstairs."

Her body changes. I see it happen. When she's talking to me, every muscle is tensed up. As if she's doing her best not to flinch. But when that dog's involved, she turns into a soggy dishcloth.

"Really?" she whispers. "You taught Alaska how to do that? To press the alarm with her nose when you have a seizure?"

"Yep. At first I had a camera in my bedroom. It was always on. It had a motion sensor, so if I suddenly started shaking when I was doing my homework or asleep, then my mom and dad would hear a beeping sound."

She waits.

"Can you imagine what that's like?" I ask. "Never being allowed to be alone? Your mom and dad always watching you with a camera?"

The holes in the balaclava stare at me.

"Yes," she says quietly. "I can imagine." She kneels back down by the beast. "And now Alaska's the camera. Wow."

I want to laugh at her. She's acting like that dog is the cleverest circus animal ever. And at the same time I want to kick something, because I can see how much she's missed the hairy monster. Her hands can't stop stroking it.

I'm certain that if the world was ending now, she'd go on stroking. Right the way through all the tsunamis.

"Are you allergic to dogs?" I ask. "That was all Yvonne told us. That's why Alaska had to leave her old owners."

The girl shakes her head. "Not me—my six-year-old brother. We thought he had a cold all winter. But he didn't. He was allergic."

"And the beast had to go."

"Or Joey had to go," she says. "But my mom and dad wanted to keep him. And so it was Alaska who went."

I snort, but she's silent. I can't see her face, of course. But I'd bet quite a bit of money that she's not laughing at her own joke.

"And now I need to get going," she says. Her hand is still stroking away. "Or my mom and dad will notice I'm missing."

"I don't even know your name!" I want to talk louder, but I keep whispering.

It's a miracle my mom and dad still haven't heard anything. But ever since the beast arrived, they've slept like logs. It's hardly surprising. They've had a whole year of sleepless nights.

We've read plenty about it online. Some epileptic people have a seizure at night and suffocate on their pillow. Others fall out of bed, slash open an artery and bleed to death.

"Can I come back to visit?" the girl asks hesitantly. "Not tomorrow night, but the night after? Will you be here?"

So it really is a dream.

Asking if I might just happen to be in my own bed later this week in the middle of the night!

"Is that a date?" I ask.

But she doesn't reply. She's only got eyes for the hairy monster. It seems to have another five hundred places that need stroking.

"I'll come back," she whispers. Not to me, but to the beast. "I promise. I'll come back."

*   *   *

Wow.

Imagine a girl talking to you like that. Saying *I'll come back*—and sounding like she'll die if she never sees you again.

You couldn't take it seriously, of course. Girls always overdo everything, their voices are too high, they *simply adore* horses and glitter, and they act all secretive about bras.

But it must be kind of nice. If someone's not talking to an animal like that, but to you.

And then she's gone. The doors slide shut. The windows glint. I don't even see her walk away.

PARKER

I don't dare wear my blue trainers to school. What if Sven remembers seeing exactly the same sneakers last night? Then he'll know who I am. So I put on my sandals instead. And a skirt, because the heatwave isn't over yet.

I've slept two hours less than usual, but I feel more awake than ever. My hair dances in the wind, and my legs pedal as if they could keep on going forever. When I spot that man and his dog again on the last long street before school, I start smiling. I wave at them, even though I don't know them.

Last night I didn't dream about Alaska—for the first time in four months. Last night I hugged her for real. I know it wasn't a dream because this morning the balaclava and my polo neck were covered in white hairs. I buried them deep under my mattress. Tomorrow night I can go again. And until then I have to pretend there's nothing going on.

It feels weird, being back in the classroom with Sven.

Everything's different now: it's broad daylight, not three in the morning. We're at school, not in his bedroom. I'm not wearing a balaclava, he's not almost naked, and his voice sounds like a big old bulldozer and not like a funny little hedgehog.

And here, in the classroom, he knows my name.

"Hey, Parker!" he yells. "What are you going to bark for us today? Can you rap like a dog too?"

At first, when he shouts my name across the room, I think he's just overdoing the English pronunciation. People do that sometimes. *Paaarkurr*—like they've got a hot meatball in their mouths. But then I suddenly hear it, along with the rest of the class.

He didn't call me Parker. He called me *Barker*.

I've had loads of nicknames in my life, but never one that went straight through my heart. The only way to kill werewolves is with silver bullets. Well, today Sven Beekman came up with a silver bullet just for me. Barker.

I stare at him in silence, while the class goes crazy. *Parker the Barker! Ms Barker Montijn!*

Sven glances back with his ice-blue eyes.

Inside my head I hear the funny little hedgehog asking, *Is that a date?* But in the real world I hate him.

I wish I'd managed to kidnap Alaska. I wish we were on our way together to Paris or Antarctica, because that boy doesn't deserve a dog to keep him alive. Sven Beekman deserves to choke on his own tongue.

When school's finally over, I'm still so angry that I accidentally end up looking like my brothers. I'm not walking. I'm marching. And suddenly I think: *Today I feel brave enough to go to the store.* If I bump into someone with a balaclava or a knife or a gun, I'll just think of the silver bullet he invented for me. And then I'll beat the bad guy to a pulp.

I leave my bike at the end of the shopping street. I clench my fists so my fingers don't shake, and I try to remember details of the people I see, but among all those shoppers I just keep seeing Sven's ice-blue eyes.

A bald man walks past. The black letters on his T-shirt say: *THINK. FEEL. DO.* A furious thought flashes through me: *Seriously, which of the three would you forget to do if it wasn't written on your belly?* He scratches his shiny, sweaty dome, and I wonder to myself if men are actually dumber than women. They're certainly more criminal. Look at the prisons. I googled it: eight percent of prisoners are women. Ninety-two percent are men.

I don't get why that's not reported on the news more often. Why they don't give boys extra classes at school. Why they don't just ban men from going out after sunset.

The window of Montijn Photographic Supplies looks the same way it has all my life. Shiny cameras and lenses displayed on rows of shelves.

The door is open. I reach the doorway and come to a stop. My body refuses to go any further.

Things that look exactly the same can suddenly feel completely different.

From the doorway I look at my mom. She's behind the counter, bent over a camera. There are no customers inside. New security cameras are hanging all over the place. I give the one facing the door a quick wave for my dad. I know he's at home, watching the black-and-white pictures on the computer. That's what he's been doing for five weeks now.

Then my mom notices me.

"Parker!" She smiles, but still a shiver runs through me. I'm sure she remembers her own daughter's name, but I still heard her say *Barker*.

"Why don't you come outside?" I ask. "It's boiling in there!"

I know she understands. She carefully puts down the camera.

There's a brightly colored poster by the till. *Armed robbery!* it says. *Always take CARE! Don't forget the CARE code!*

I know the words by heart:

C: *Stay **Calm**.*
A: ***Accept** what's happening. Don't resist.*
R: ***Remember** what they look like.*
E: *Give them **Everything** they ask for.*

I used to think the poster meant it would all be fine. As long as you followed the letters, you'd be OK. But that's not how it works. There's no such thing as OK. *Not dying*—that's what it's all about. When *dead* is the alternative, *not dead* sounds pretty good.

My mom and I lean against the doorposts. As if we're guards. We have the same straight, light-brown hair, the same freck-led nose, the same gray eyes. On the outside I'm my mom, but inside I'm my dad. Dad and I are the cowards. Mom and my brothers are the brave ones.

It's muggy out on the street. The sun's disappeared and there's a storm in the air. I look at the shoes of every man who goes by. Shoes are the most important thing of all.

"How was school?" asks my mom.

"OK," I say.

"Want some Fanta?"

I nod.

She goes in to fetch two cans from the fridge at the back of the store. While I'm waiting outside, I automatically look down at my phone to check if there's another message from my mom.

There's nothing, of course. It's only as I'm staring at the screen that I realize how dumb I am. I'm here. And Mom's already coming back out. Right now, I can be certain that she's still alive. Safe and sound, she leans on the warm wall beside me.

SVEN

I'm not a caveman. But if I was, then last night I'd have been certain the world was coming to an end. There was a massive storm.

Outside, disco lights were flashing and mountains were smashing into each other. Inside, the beast lay shivering next to my bed. Dogs and cavemen are sort of in the same situation. Lots of raw bones. Not much access to the online weather forecast.

When the light show was directly above our heads, I finally gave in. For the rest of the night, the hairy monster lay right up against me.

And now I'm awake, even though it's only half past six.

I dreamed about the girl in the balaclava. With the thunder booming in the background, we were driving together in a Porsche 911 Carrera on a winding road along a steep coast. The kind of road that makes you think: *If there's one place I never want to have an epileptic seizure, then it's here.*

But the crickets were chirping away, and I could drive like

a pro. And she was sitting beside me, smiling. No idea how I knew that, because even in my dream she was wearing that balaclava. With the wonky eyes and the triangular mouth.

She's coming back tonight. At least that's what she said.

Still in bed, I look around my room.

In the gray morning light, I suddenly see what a tip it is. Dirty socks, comic books, sneakers, a broken drone, the helmet I only wore once and then never again—because I'd rather drop down dead than walk around looking like an idiot with that on my head for the rest of my life.

And another few hundred bits of junk.

Suddenly I wonder what Balaclava Girl thought of the mess. Was she just looking at Alaska? Or did she spot that tub of moldy dip too?

I rub my eyes, throw back the quilt and get out of bed.

While I'm tidying up, Alaska sticks really close to me. After a while, she starts whimpering and nudging my leg with her nose.

What's up with the beast? Is she laughing at me because I've finally started to clear up the chaos?

"Yep, I agree," I say to her. "I must be nuts."

*   *   *

You see?

I really am nuts. Look at me, standing here like some lonely old cat lady, talking to my pet. Any m i n u t e   n o w   I

PARKER

Sven isn't at school today.

I can relax a bit, because no one comes up with any new jokes about Parker the Barker all day. But at the same time I keep thinking: *What's going to happen tonight?* He could have had one of those seizures where his face goes blue and they had to take him to hospital. Then he won't have left the door open a bit, and I'll be stuck outside in the dark. With my nose pressed up against the glass. And Alaska going crazy inside.

When I get out of bed at 2:00 A.M., I have instant goose-bumps. Yesterday's storm put an end to the summer. Of course it's ridiculous to go sneaking back into Sven's house in the middle of the night. But it's my only option.

My mom and dad say I can't see Alaska again. They say it would be unkind to visit her at her new place. She wouldn't understand. We couldn't explain to her why she had to leave. And if we suddenly appear again, she'll be completely confused.

I know that, but here I am anyway, cycling along the gleaming streets. Everything is different from five weeks ago. My body feels like it's slowly crumbling away. Without Alaska, there soon won't be anything left of me. Look at my dad. He used to be a human being. And now he's just empty packaging.

Other people can be sensible if they like, but I've had enough of that. I'm finally doing what all those websites keep telling me to do: I'm being myself. And I, Parker the Barker, need to see Alaska.

I put on the balaclava before climbing over the fence. The wet wood is slippery under my hands. My heart is thumping even harder than before, because this time I know what's going to happen: I'm not just on my way to Alaska, but also to Sven. If everything's OK, if he's not in hospital, if the door is slightly open, then I'm going to have to talk to him again.

The door is open.

As I feel for the handle in the dark, Alaska is already quietly starting to sing. And as soon as I step into the room, the bedside lamp goes on. I blink. Sven is sitting up in bed—as if he was waiting for me. This time he isn't almost naked. He's wearing a dark T-shirt and his blond hair is falling over his forehead. There's a bandage on his left hand.

"You're here!" I whisper.

He raises his eyebrows. "Shouldn't I be saying that to you?"

Feeling a bit dizzy, I crouch down to pet Alaska. I need to be really careful now. To whisper as quietly as possible, so that he doesn't recognize my voice. And to remember that I don't know a thing about him. I don't know he wasn't at school today, I don't know that he makes up nasty nicknames, and I don't even know what color his eyes are. You can't see that by the light of his bedside lamp.

I sit on the floor. Last time it was covered in junk, but now his room has been tidied. Alaska is jumping around me, licking my neck and swishing her tail into my face. I whisper nonsense, just because it's so good to talk to her again.

"Are you a happy puppy, Alassie? Are you good at singing?"

"You call that singing?" whispers Sven from his bed. "You should come to my school. There's a girl in my new class who can bark 'Jingle Bells'."

I freeze.

"She's called Parker," says Sven. "Parker, the amazing barking girl! So now I call her Barker."

Inside my throat, there are two of those drawstrings that you use to close a gym bag. Sven is holding them firmly in his hands. And he's pulling them.

"Get it?" he asks. "Barker. Woof!"

I clench my fists.

"Of course I get it," I whisper. "I'm not stupid."

"But you're not laughing."

"I don't happen to find bullying very funny."

"But didn't you hear what I said?" he asks. "That girl started *barking*. So it's OK to call her Barker, isn't it?"

I just want to get away. But I can't, because I still have to pet Alaska. It's like in the tales of *One Thousand and One Nights*. As long as I keep talking calmly to Sven, he won't give me away to his mom and dad. As long as I listen to his horrid stories, I can keep on stroking Alaska.

So I pretend that I'm someone else. A girl who comes from the other side of the planet. I have never, ever barked for a single second in my entire life. I don't know anyone called Parker the Barker.

"What happened to your hand?" I ask, pointing at the bandage.

"Bruised it." He sighs. "I had another seizure this morning."

"Did Alaska press the alarm button?"

"Yes, she saved my life again. I was standing here in my room and suddenly I went crashing to the floor. Right on top of my hand. And then I almost choked, so they had to call an ambulance."

He brushes the hair off his forehead and stares at the bandage.

"I am *so* tired of this. It's been going on for a year now. And if we don't find the right medication, then it's never going to stop."

The big old bulldozer has vanished from his voice. The funny little hedgehog too.

"The only people I've seen today have been parents and doctors," he says gloomily. "The past few weeks had been all right. The move was out of the way, and the dog classes were going OK. But then there was my new school and my new class, and my dumb epilepsy gets worse when I'm stressed."

"Stressed?" I ask in surprise.

"Yes, stressed!" He frowns. "What year are you in?"

"Second," I whisper. All I can think is: *I'm not Parker the Barker. I'm not in the first year. I'm someone completely different.*

"So you must remember what it was like to go to a new school. I get lost half of the time, I don't understand any French, and my whole class has a panic attack when I have a seizure. And I have to give talks about epilepsy all the time." He sighs. "Imagine walking around on Mars for the rest of your life. And having to explain how you work to every Martian you meet: how you breathe, how your nose runs, how you pee, how you puke—and every time they go 'ooh' and 'ah' and look at you as if *you're* the alien." He shrugs. "That's my life. But I don't have to go to Mars for it."

As I look at him, I can hardly believe that the idiot in my class is really the boy who's sitting there in that bed.

"I had..." He stops and irritably brushes the hair off his forehead again.

"What?" I ask. "What did you have?"

"Never mind."

There are dark circles under his eyes. The cut on his chin has only just healed and now he's got a bruised hand too.

Just imagine, I think. *Just imagine suddenly hearing that you've got to live on Mars for the rest of your life.*

"Tell me," I say. Quietly, as if I'm talking to Alaska.

He sighs. "I had this plan all worked out. On that very first morning, I was going to pull off a brilliant stunt. So that the whole school would hear about me. And not about Sven the alien who lies there drooling and shaking, but about Sven who—well, you know..." He shrugs. "I couldn't actually come up with anything. And I was too much of a coward. I was walking through the halls all on my own, and suddenly I felt really terrified that I'd have a seizure."

Alaska is lying next to me now, on her side. Her legs stretched out, her back against my thigh. My hand is stroking the warm, dry pads on her paws. Sleepily, she nudges my leg with her head. Sometimes I can hardly believe that dogs and people can love each other so much.

"What you wanted on Monday..." I don't look at Sven. "That's what *everyone* wants. To do something amazing, so that the whole school immediately knows who you are. Or, even better—the whole world. But does it ever happen? No, of course not! And that's nothing to do with your epilepsy."

He doesn't say anything. At any moment, he could make another joke about the girl who barked, but right now he's silent.

"It's only the first week," I whisper. "What were you expecting? That you were Harry Potter? That you'd get to school and everyone would say they'd been waiting for you for years? And that you're going to save the world?"

He snorts. "Well, it would be pretty cool."

"Yeah? Well, I'm not interested in all that," I say.

"Really?"

"No! I don't want to save the world. The world can't be saved."

"Is that right?" he asks. "The bad guys are going to win, are they?"

I swallow. "They already have."

Silently, I lie down beside Alaska. My arms around her body, my face in her fur.

There are no prisons for animals, because animals are never bad. If they eat each other, it's only because they have no other choice. Because there are no bowls of biscuits out there on the savannah. Animals aren't especially good either—they just *are*. They are *themselves*, just like all those websites want you to be.

But suddenly I realize that Alaska is different now. She has a job as an assistance dog. She doesn't get paid for it, she won't become famous, she won't get extra tasty snacks or a golden collar. But, even so, she's helping a human being.

"Now you," says Sven.

"Now me what?" I ask.

"Now you have to tell me something. I don't know anything about you."

I don't reply.

"Or you could take off that balaclava," he says. "That would count."

I bury my hands deep in Alaska's fur, so that I can touch her warm skin. Her fur is a bit too big for her body. It's like she's wearing a furry onesie. It feels baggy under her chin.

"You have three options," says Sven. "One: tell me something. Two: take off that balaclava. Three: I'll press the alarm button. If my mom and dad hear that Alaska used to belong to you, then you'll never be allowed to come back here. They take the rules for assistance dogs pretty seriously. No one's allowed to distract her—and certainly not her old owner."

Now I hate him again.

So it really is *One Thousand and One Nights*. I have to talk, or it stops here and now. And that can't be allowed to happen.

Never seeing Alaska again—that is not an option. I've been trying for four months now, but I don't miss her any less. Only more.

I clench my fists.

There is actually only one story I can tell. No one at school knows what happened this summer—and that includes Sven. I've never told anyone about it—at least not normal people anyway. Just the police.

"Well?" he says. "Have you fallen asleep?"

I sit up straight.

SVEN

"It all happened five weeks ago," the girl in the balaclava says quietly.

It sounds as if she's about to start telling me a fairy tale.

I rest my bruised paw on the quilt and wait for her to continue. I still haven't seen her face, but I feel as if I know her.

Or more like she knows me.

It's really stupid. I say things to her that I don't say to anyone else.

My psychologist is always whining that I don't tell him anything. So next time I'll tell him to put a balaclava over his head. And that it might be a good idea to turn off the light.

"My mom and dad have a store..."

Balaclava Girl was lying next to Alaska, but now she's sitting up again. Six feet from my bed. Her arms around her knees, her fists clenched tight.

"The store was there before I was born. One night, years ago, there was a break-in. But there'd never been an armed robbery. Not until this summer."

She looks at the beast. "It's so weird...Alaska doesn't know anything about it. It happened after she'd gone. She only knows us the way we were before the robbery."

I want to say something funny. To ask if we should put our hands over her doggy ears to prevent the hairy monster from having nightmares.

But I keep my mouth shut.

"I was there," says the girl. "I saw it all. The security camera filmed it, but I was there too. I was in the office at the back of the store, and I saw it happen."

"You saw your mom and dad being robbed?"

She nods. "I hid behind the coats on the rack. But I could still see the store through the coat sleeves."

The beast awakes and sits up. She's listening. Her front legs stretched out, her face serious, as if she understands every word.

"It was late-night shopping, so we were going to shut at nine. They came in at seven minutes to. Two men in black, with balaclavas on their heads."

I look at the thing on the girl's head, and really don't get it. So why's she wearing a balaclava? Why does she insist on keeping it on?

"The smaller man had a knife in his hand. The tall one had a gun." She looks at me through those staring holes in her balaclava. "Have you ever seen a gun in real life?"

I shake my head, and she shrugs.

"It looks exactly like you think. Exactly like in the movies."

I don't say anything. I'd quite like to see a Glock 9mm for real.

"They yelled at them to open the till. My dad just turned to stone. He didn't do a thing. Which I could understand, because I didn't do anything either. My mom shouted back at them and said there wasn't any money. That they'd just taken it to the bank. And then the tall man hit the side of her head with his gun."

She clasps her hands together.

"My mom opened the till. I saw some blood running down her cheek, just a thin little trickle. And I saw the shoes of the man with the gun. Black, with red flames on the sides of the soles."

She clears her throat.

"Suddenly my dad could move again. And then he came up with the bright idea of pressing the alarm button. That red button you have beside your bed? Well, they've got them in the store too. But when you press the button, it's not parents who come. It's the police."

"Good for your dad!" I say.

She shakes her head furiously. "No! It was incredibly dumb! You're not supposed to press the button until after they've gone. Not while the robbery is still going on. Before he'd even reached the button, they shot him. And then they ran. I don't think they could stand the sight of blood."

She leans over Alaska and starts stroking her again. As if the story's over.

I don't want to ask, but I can't stop myself.

"So...is he still alive? Your dad?"

She shrugs. "Sort of."

Seriously. What kind of answer is that when someone's asked if your dad's still alive? Shrugging your shoulders, like it doesn't matter? Who does that?

"No one is *sort of* alive," I say, more angrily than I mean to.

She sighs. "He was hit in the shoulder. When the ambulance took him away, there was this big puddle of blood on the floor. Three days later, he was allowed to leave hospital. And now he's at home."

"So it all turned out OK."

She sighs again. "Sort of. The blood soaked into the floor, so there's still a stain. And now he sits at home all day, just staring at the computer, watching the live feed from the security cameras, because he's too scared to go to the store now."

"And what about your mom?"

"Yeah, she still goes in. The store was only closed for a weekend. She says we can't let the bad guys win. She doesn't want to be afraid."

"That's brave," I say—and the girl shakes her head again.

"No! She's incredibly dumb too! Those robbers are still walking around free. And there are all those other criminals out there as well. Any day there could be another robbery. Any day someone on the street could beat you up. Any day someone on your bus could blow themselves up. It could happen at any time. Any minute. Any second."

She curls up small. Her shoulders shake, and she puts her hand over her mouth.

Alaska is busily licking away at her other hand, like she does with me after a fit.

The beast must be thinking: *Seizures? Robberies? What can I do? I'll lie here. I'll give them a bit of a lick.*

I pause for what must be a hundred seconds, and then I get out of bed.

I mean, she won't stop crying, so what else am I supposed to do?

I carefully sit down on the floor beside her. I've never comforted a girl in my life.

Never mind "a girl." I've never comforted *anyone* before.

"I don't get it," she says in a hoarse voice.

Her tears are rolling straight into the balaclava. I can't see them.

"How do people do it? How do they just go on with their lives when they know everything could go wrong at any moment?"

I look up at the helmet that I put on top of my closet this morning. The doctors wanted me to wear it all the time. Yeah, right.

My unbruised hand slowly moves to her shoulder.

The moment I touch her, she shivers. But she stays sitting there. With my hand on her shoulder.

And now? What happens next?

Imagine if I wanted to comfort Alaska—yeah, just imagine that—then obviously I'd stroke her. Simple. My hand doesn't need to come up with anything complicated: brush half a foot to the left, then half a foot to the right. And repeat that about thirty times.

A dog I can handle. But what do you do with a girl's shoulder?

"Can I come back on Friday night?" she asks quietly.

"Fine by me," I say.

She stands up, and my hand falls off her shoulder.

She gives Alaska a bit more of a stroke, because everyone can pet dogs. Half a foot to the left, half a foot to the right—piece of cake.

PARKER

The next morning, everyone in 1B obviously wants to know why Sven wasn't at school yesterday. It's at least a quarter of an hour before our math class can start. Everyone sits listening breathlessly to his story about his major seizure, the wailing ambulance, the bruised hand and the blond nurse who took his blood.

I watch in silence. Not through the holes in my balaclava, but just normally, with my eyes. Last night I looked at his face for at least an hour. And now I can see everything at once. I can see the big old bulldozer, and also the funny little hedgehog. And even when he's grinning away and telling the story about the nurse, I can see the ordinary human boy who's stuck on Mars for the rest of his life. The boy who has to explain every day how he breathes.

At lunchtime, I get a text message from my mom. Something is up with Finn. There's nothing to worry about, but when my brothers get picked up from school, his teacher would like to have a quick word with Dad.

I call Mom right away.

"I'll go with Dad," I say.

"Really? Would you do that?" She sounds worried. "I tried to see if Erik could stand in for me, but he's already coming in tonight. I really can't leave the store."

"I'll make sure I'm at their school at half past two."

"Can you do that? Don't you have class?"

"No, it's a short day."

She doesn't know my timetable yet, of course. She doesn't know that 1B have class until half three today.

"Thanks, Parker. That's a load off my mind."

In biology, the others are learning the difference between living, non-living and dead, but all I can think is: *What's up with Finn?*

When the bell finally goes, I don't walk off with the rest of them. I have to go and report myself sick. It's none of the school's business how my family works so, from this moment on, I have a bad case of flu.

I see Sven walking through the empty hall, ahead of me. He's on his way to the elevator, all on his own. His feet are dragging along the floor, and I look at his black T-shirt. Was he wearing the same one last night? Is he really wearing his bed T-shirt to school?

I want to think it's grubby, but I can't quite manage it. And I can't seem to forget his hand on my shoulder either. I don't understand how it can feel so different—being touched by Alaska, or by Sven.

Is it because of Alaska's fur? When she nudges me with her head, it's like being cuddled by a teddy bear. But when Sven put his hand on my shoulder, it felt like—well, it felt like being touched by a *person*.

This is the first time I've walked across the primary-school playground without belonging there. My dad's waiting on the bench under the chestnut tree. His face is gray, and his head looks like a crumpled-up ball of paper. The shoulder they shot is lower than the other one.

I bite my lip. So now I have to talk to him. To walk along beside him, where everyone can see. For a moment, I wish I had a different dad. A bulldozer, not a ball of paper. But I already regret thinking that.

"We've been back at school four days now," says Finn's teacher with a serious look on her face, "and in that time Finn has kicked five of his classmates, tied up two of the infants, and today he hit seven children on the head with a stick."

"It wasn't a stick," says Finn. "It was my gun."

Dex and Joey play outside while Dad, Finn and I talk to the teacher. She's new, so I don't know her. The chairs we're sitting on are low, and the tables are sticky. Welcome to primary school.

"So, of course, I spoke to Finn about his conduct," she says.

I wonder if that's something you learn at teaching school. To say you spoke to someone about their conduct.

"And then he told me that he's a soldier. Not just at school, but at home. In fact, he said that it's all part of his upbringing. That he has to march every day and go out on missions, or he doesn't get any dinner."

"Hmm," says Dad. His face is even grayer than before.

"How strange," I say. "I'll talk to him. That's clearly not acceptable."

"Indeed." The teacher looks stern. "Luckily there haven't been any serious accidents yet. But we've had a split lip and a couple of bruises. And obviously I know that you've all had a tough summer. But Finn's behavior really does need to improve."

Dad and I nod enthusiastically. I give Finn a kick under the table, and then he nods enthusiastically too.

"We'll give him a good talking-to," I say. That sounds like the sort of thing you might learn at parenting school.

When we're all around the corner and the school is no longer in sight, I yell: "Soldiers! Atten-TION!" I look at Joey and whisper: "That means you have to listen."

They immediately stand in line.

"Private Finn!" I say sternly. "Why did you hit other children on the head with a stick?"

"That was not a stick, General!" Finn says, standing perfectly straight, his chin in the air. "That was my gun, General!"

I nod. "A good point, Private. Why did you hit the other children on the head with your gun?"

"They were the bad guys, General! They had knives and pistols! So I gave them a clobbering!"

As I look at them standing there in a line, I want to hug them. My own private army, with their messy hair and their hands that look like they've just dug a tunnel to Australia.

"Listen carefully," I shout. "All the kids at your school are soldiers too! You are all in the same army. There are no bad guys at school, only fellow soldiers. Private Finn, do you understand that you must not hit other soldiers on the head? Do you understand that your mission is to protect them?"

"Yes, General! I will protect them, General!" He wrinkles his nose. "What about the teacher?"

"Seriously?" I say. "Did you hit your teacher on the head too?"

"Couldn't reach, General! She was too tall, General!"

I see my dad's face relax, just for a moment. And then he starts looking around again, as if he's searching for the alarm button.

"Your teacher," I say seriously to Finn, "is your—um—colonel, so you must listen to her. And Private Joey and Private Dex, your teachers are your colonels too. Is that understood, soldiers?"

"Yes, General!"

"Good. Diiiis-missed! March!"

They salute, turn ninety degrees and start marching away.

Dad and I follow them in silence. And suddenly I think: *If only it were tomorrow night. I want to tell Sven what just happened.*

SVEN

Yvonne's coming round for a training session. The beast's already in her harness. She's so happy that she's dancing.

I thought I'd be in a foul mood: first a whole week at school and then another full hour of dog classes on Friday afternoon. But I'm not in a foul mood at all, because this morning I suddenly realized: Yvonne knows who Alaska's previous owner was.

She knows Balaclava Girl.

Dogs don't pay any attention to appearances—Yvonne is the living proof of that. She's absolutely huge and she wears at least five different colors at the same time. But yeah, the beast adores her.

As soon as Yvonne comes in, Alaska starts acting like the best assistance dog in the universe. And the really dumb thing is: I can see why she wants to please her. Yvonne is the boss—you can feel it.

You get all those guys in their smart suits, trying to look all tough. But Yvonne just stands there. Feet firmly on the ground as if they have roots. Completely relaxed. And you do whatever she tells you to do.

First we go outside to practice "Alaska, sit!" and "Alaska, let's go!" And walking nicely without pulling on the leash. Yvonne says it's mainly me who needs to learn how to do that.

I still can't stand being put on display next to that assistance-dog vest. Everyone always asks questions. And even though the vest says, *DO NOT PET* in big letters, people still start cooing away at the beast: "Oh, I know I'm not supposed to pet you, but you're so sweet. How can I resist? Ha ha."

It is very simple: you have to ignore assistance dogs.

And no, that's not sad.

If you saw a policeman directing traffic, would you go and pinch his cheeks? Have you ever given the pilot of your plane a little tickle under the armpits?

Well, the beast's no different.

When she's wearing her vest, she is at work. And she could do without being prodded and poked by every idiot who comes along.

"So..." I say when we come to a long and straight section of sidewalk. "Um... Where was it that Alaska used to live?"

Yvonne raises her penciled-in eyebrows.

"Oh? So now you're suddenly curious?"

She's not just a dog whisperer, you see. She's secretly a human whisperer too. She can see right through you.

I shrug. "Just wondering. Did she, like, live with some old man or maybe with...um...*children*?"

Yvonne laughs. "Yep. Four of them, to be precise. I met the family out in the woods one day. There was a girl of about your age and three little brothers who were yelling their heads off. They said they were looking for a new home for Alaska, so I told them that I train assistance dogs to work with children. They thought it sounded like a great idea."

"The girl you mentioned..." I say. "Did she have a name?"

Yvonne stops and gives me a hard stare.

Go on, I think. *Say it!*

I've dreamed about her three times, I tell her just about everything, and she's coming again tonight.

And I still have no idea who she is.

But Yvonne shakes her head.

"Alaska's *your* dog now," she says calmly. "Her old owners hated having to say goodbye to her, but that's all in the past. Come on, we've got work to do."

"I only asked what her name was! Just her first name. You can tell me that, can't you?"

"We'll continue indoors. Have the two of you been practicing with your medicine bag?"

For the rest of the dog class, I am very grumpy.

I can't get it out of my mind: Alaska running through the woods with three boys yelling away. Without her stupid harness. Without any nasty medicine bags to carry, without tasks and commands and a job to do.

And then, of course, getting all those hugs from Balaclava Girl. Every day, nonstop, right the way through all the tsunamis.

I kick the wall, because now I'm sure of it. The beast liked living with her more than with me.

PARKER

I haven't been on a bad-guy hunt all week.

Every afternoon, I came up with some excuse or other, but now I've run out. I know "bad guy" sounds childish, but that's a good thing. When I say "bad guys," I think of clumsy cartoon characters in black-and-white striped pajamas. Not those two men in the store. The little one with the knife. The tall one who shot Dad.

I'm sitting on the wall at the end of the shopping street. With a book in my hands, but I'm not reading. I'm looking at the shoes of every man who walks by.

The police say they're doing their best. They've studied the pictures from the security camera, and what they know is this: the robbers were wearing black Adidas sweatpants, black hoodies (brand unknown) and black balaclavas. That's all they could get from the pictures. My mom didn't see anything more than that either. And no one knows what my dad saw. Not even him. There's a gap in his memory.

Over the past few weeks, I've studied hundreds of shoes walking by. Yes, of course I told the police about the black shoes with the red flames on the sides of the soles. They now know exactly which Air Jordans the tall one with the gun was wearing. But I'm the only one who knows what the shoes *really* looked like. Not fresh out of the box, but on that guy's feet.

The robbers made one big mistake. When they ran away, they pulled off their balaclavas as soon as they got outside. You see, people notice when you run down the street in disguise. They shoved their balaclavas into the pockets of their sweatpants, but one of them messed up. He dropped his balaclava.

The police found it later on the street outside the store. They compared it to the pictures and identified it as the bala-clava that the man with the gun had been wearing. There were a few of his hairs inside, so now they have his DNA.

But what good is that? You can't go around the entire country taking a little bit of DNA from every man. *Sorry, sir, we just want to find out if you're a criminal.* As long as there's no suspect, a grubby balaclava with a few hairs in it is no use at all. And that's why I'm here. On the wall. Looking at shoes.

Every thirty seconds, I'm sure I'm about to faint. That my heart's going to thump itself to pieces, and my brain will run out of blood. Every thirty seconds, I think: *I want to leave.* But I stay. I press my hands as hard as I can against the rough bricks of the wall.

Tonight I'll be able to stroke Alaska again, I tell myself. If I can keep this up for an hour, that's my reward. I don't think about Sven. Not about his blue husky eyes, not about the way he brushes his hair off his forehead, not about the way his voice sounds when he talks about his seizures.

Sometimes I glance at faces instead of shoes, but then I quickly look back down again. I just don't get it. How can all those people walk along so calmly? Their expressions not haunted, no alarm buttons anywhere nearby, the emergency number not already keyed in on their cell phones. Don't they ever watch the news?

Maybe they don't care if they're alive or dead. Or maybe they're with the bad guys too, and they're thinking: *In this world, you'd better make sure you have a gun in your hand.*

SVEN

In the middle of the night, I wake up with a start. My dozy head is suddenly perfectly clear.

I am such an idiot!

All I know about Balaclava Girl is that she's in the second year, and that she comes to my house at night on her bike. That's not enough information to find her online.

But a robbery five weeks ago, here in our town, when the store owner got shot in the shoulder, and the robbers are still on the run? Now that's something I can google.

I look at my telephone and see that it's five past two in the morning. If it's the same as last time, she'll be here in less than half an hour.

I go to Google.

It's pretty lame, I know, but I'm out of breath. And my fingers mistype three times.

I click on the magnifying glass. There it is!

ARMED ROBBERY! MONTIJN PHOTO SUPPLIES—OWNER WOUNDED

I want to go on reading, but my eyes stick on that one word: Montijn. A name I'd never heard before—until this week.

Every teacher begins every class by marking who's absent. They learn our names by repeating them thousands of times. Sven Beekman. Sol Louakili. Ziva de Vries.

Parker Montijn.

The girl who started barking in the very first class.

I look at Alaska and, in my mind, two completely different worlds slowly start to come together.

That quiet, skinny girl in my class—and the dark shadow in the balaclava. The barking girl by day—and the stroking girl by night.

It makes no sense.

I'm going round the bend. There are lots of people who have the same name.

But check this: we'd been living here all summer without Balaclava Girl ever coming round. And then Monday night, after the very first day at school, she suddenly turned up.

Is it coincidence?

I need to know. Now.

I sit up straight and look at the beast again.

Seriously, I'm actually nervous.

And then I start barking.

"Wuff wuff woof, wuff wuff woof..."

I'm barely halfway through the first line when Alaska jumps up. She runs over to me, wagging her tail, puts her front paws on my quilt and sticks her nose in the air. "Wuff, wuf, wuff, wuf, woooff!"

She can do it. She can bark "Jingle Bells."

Before I have time to think about it, my mom comes rushing in. Hair in a mess, crumpled nightie.

"Sven?" When she sees me sitting up in bed, she stops dead in her tracks. "I heard Alaska barking! I thought you..."

In my head I see the holes in the balaclava staring at me.

So there is no mysterious girl smiling at me as we drive on a winding road along a steep coast.

The eyes of Parker from 1B have been behind those black holes all along.

"What's going on?" asks my mom. "Why was Alaska barking?"

I brush the hair out of my eyes, silently swearing to myself. There's a girl in my class who knows everything about me...

"Sven? What's wrong?"

I hold up my phone. "I was playing a game on my phone because I couldn't sleep. But the sound was on, and the beast suddenly starting barking along."

It's one of those wonderful moments when you can really shine as a mother. When you're certain that you're right and that hundreds of scientists and academics would back you up. Because after staring at an illuminated screen, I obviously won't be able to get to sleep. And if I don't get enough sleep, I'll have extra seizures, and then...

Oh. My. God, is all I can think. *Just go away! Any moment now, we'll be here having our Educational Moment when Balaclava Girl —*

No, not Balaclava Girl.

Parker.

When Parker the Barker gets here.

I clench my fists.

She's known who I am the entire time. She looked at me through the holes in her balaclava and saw me lying there half naked in my boxers. She listened to my stories about the failed stunt, she let me comfort her, she stroked Alaska.

Woah, it feels like she's seen my *brain* half naked. My sparking brain full of short circuits, in nothing but its underwear.

*   *   *

Before long she'll be standing here again beside my bed in her black disguise. And suddenly I know what I'm going to do: I won't tell her that I've found out. She thinks she has a secret— well, she doesn't. I might be the alien with the bruised hand who's going to stay in 1B for the rest of his life, but tonight, I'm the winner.

I know everything. And Parker Montijn does not.

PARKER

For the first time, the dark streets aren't empty.

It's Friday night, and it's not just thieves who are out and about, but people who want to have fun. Groups of drunken cyclists sway and swerve along the road, and my hands immediately start shaking again.

The TV news tonight went on about a bomb for ten minutes. A car bomb in a town square full of people. Thirteen dead, a hundred wounded, pools of blood that they just covered up with sand.

My dad leaves the room as soon as the news begins, but my mom watches without batting an eyelid. Even when they say, *Some of these images might be disturbing.* Or maybe especially then. She knows someone still has to be there. Someone who watches. Someone who goes to the store. Someone who takes care of us.

I sat beside Mom on the sofa and stared at the screaming people on TV. I tried to keep track of what was going on, because if you stop paying attention for just a second, you can't tell whether you're looking at the good guys or the bad guys.

*   *   *

Behind me, in the dark, I hear someone shout.

"Hey, sweetheart! Where are you off to at this time of night?"

I glance over my shoulder. Two men, laughing.

"Aren't you a bit young to be going to the pub?" shouts the other one.

I start cycling faster.

They probably don't have guns. They probably won't do anything to me. But how can you tell who's going to shoot and who's on his way to visit his grandma?

I'm panting when I enter Sven's room. I slide the doors shut behind me as quickly as possible and pull down the handle with a jerk. Out of breath, I stroke Alaska.

"What's up? Someone chasing you?" Sven asks coolly.

He's not sitting in his bed, but on his chair, with his feet up on the desk. He's wearing a hoodie and looking at me in a way I don't understand. As Alaska dances around me, I quickly reach up to touch the balaclava—no, he can't see my face.

"Some drunk men started yelling at me."

Alaska's warm tongue licks my hands. Her black eyes are glowing in the white. What makes dogs so great is the way they never get tired of you. They never think: *I've already seen that Parker girl twice this week, so we've run out of things to say.*

"Oh, really?" Sven still sounds just as chilly as he looks. "What were they yelling?"

"They asked where I was off to at this time of night. And if I wasn't a bit young for the pub."

He raises his eyebrows. "Oh? So they were sensible drunk men, were they?"

I don't say anything.

I lay Alaska's ear flat on my hand and stroke it with my fingertips. A thin piece of dog, as soft as can be.

"Of all the people in prison," I whisper, "ninety-two percent are men. And only eight percent are women. And it's even worse with armed robbery. Just about every single armed robber is male." I look up. The light on his desk is on, and his blond hair is glowing. "Did you know that?"

"No," he says. And then he shrugs. "So what?"

The way he's sitting there—it reminds me of a movie. Or of lots of movies: the villain at the center of his web, completely in control, giving orders for people to be murdered, while he sits there casually, with his feet up on his desk.

"So what?" I hiss. "I just don't get why we seem to think it's normal for men to kill and steal and to blow people up."

"Think about it," says Sven. "One hundred percent of Dutch prime ministers have been men. It was men who invented computers and airplanes. They discovered gravity and figured out how evolution works. We've been running the world for thousands of years—so yes, sometimes we get things wrong."

"We?"

"Yes. We! Men! At least we do something. If you don't ever do anything, you'll never end up in prison. Makes sense, doesn't it?"

He's sitting there, looking like he's running the whole world right now. The red alarm button is gleaming. It looks like the buzzer in a TV quiz show. The one that contestants have to bash when they think they know the answer.

Sven would bash it harder than anyone else. Even if he had no idea of the answer.

"Come on," he suddenly says. "We're going outside."

I stare at him. "Outside?"

"Yes, my mom was just in here. She'd heard Alaska barking. I keep thinking that we shouldn't be talking this loud— and it's annoying me."

He stands up. As soon as Alaska sees that he's putting his shoes on, she goes crazy.

"Yes, beast," he says to her. "You can come too."

I sit on the floor, frozen. We're going outside? Now, right this moment? No way. I have to whisper, or he'll recognize my voice. And I certainly don't want to go out for a walk with Sven the bulldozer in the middle of the night.

But I can hardly stay behind in his bedroom by myself.

Sven slides the door open. "We'll go out into the field at the back."

"But Alaska can't get over the fence, can she?" I whisper.

"I've got a key for the gate."

It feels like he's asking me to jump into a black hole. A black hole full of bad guys and bombs and gravity. But in the end I can't resist. The thought of it: going out with Alaska in the middle of the night. Running around together across that enormous field. Playing with a stick—and pretending she's still my dog.

SVEN

My head is about to explode. We need to get as far away as possible from the houses, so that I can scream.

I've never felt like such a fool.

Yes, slowly surfacing after a seizure—that sucks big time. Shocked faces all around, while I'm confused, trying to puzzle out what just happened, if I've hurt myself, where I am, who's with me—that's a nightmare.

But this time I didn't have a seizure. I was there, I was fully aware, I was talking to her—I can remember everything.

And she completely conned me. While I was lying there in my bed. Half naked. I told her I was too much of a coward to pull off a stunt at school. I told her that I feel like a boy on Mars who has to keep explaining how he pees.

And the next day she just sat there in class, as if nothing had happened.

We sneak through the dark yard as if there's a war on. Alaska knows exactly what's going on. The three of us are playing a game together—and in this game no one's allowed to bark.

I open the gate and let the beast and the liar out. She wants to hold Alaska's leash and that's fine by me. It's the last time she'll ever see that dog.

High above us, there's a perfectly round moon in a deep blue sky. The wind is blowing. Autumn is on its way.

"You know something?" I whisper, because the houses are still much too close. "Seems like it must be pretty hard, hating half of the world's population. Do you hate the boys in your class that much too?"

"Absolutely," she says in a flash.

"Oh really?" I ask, as if we're talking about the weather. "Why's that?"

She sighs. "They keep shoving and thumping each other all the time. They're always talking about other boys who play games on YouTube and acting like they're all funny and tough. But they're just childish bullies."

"All of them?"

"One of them in particular."

I can't see her face, of course, but I can feel her holding back.

She's walking across the bare field beside me, and her whole body is hesitant. She mustn't give herself away—but at the same time she wants nothing more than to tell me all about this one bully.

"My whole class thinks I'm stupid," she whispers. "They're laughing at me and it's all because of one boy." She kicks the sand. "Honestly, I don't feel any need to be special. I don't expect people to start cheering when I enter the room. But I don't want to be the class clown either. I accidentally did something weird just once, and now they all think I'm an idiot."

"Alaska's allowed off the leash here," I say in a cold voice.

We're away from the houses now. Grass is beginning to grow, even a few bushes. If they don't start building soon, there's going to be a whole wood here before long.

I put my hands in the pockets of my sweatpants, and I look up. Without streetlights, you can see the universe.

And here we go—she's off again. Parker the Barker, who thinks the entire world is rotten, all except for her.

Now that I know, I can recognize her voice. Even when she's whispering.

"I just don't get it," she whines. "Why so many people are bad. Why they bully and steal and murder and lie..."

"You're asking me? That's nice!" I give the ground a good kick. Really hard, so that sand sprays up all around. "I'm not the one who's been lying for a week. That's you. You've known who I was right from the beginning."

She stops, perfectly still. In the moonlight, even the holes in the balaclava are black.

"Come on, Barker!" I yell. "Bark 'Jingle Bells' again. That's your favorite hobby, isn't it?"

I think she's actually stopped breathing.

I wonder what I'll do if she passes out. I don't have my cell phone, and the alarm button's a long way away.

*   *   *

And I don't know what I'll do if I have a seizure now either.

Well, yeah, I do—not a thing. I won't know what's going on anyway.

It's a bit like being dead. But the advantage of being dead is that you don't wake up again after a while, covered in drool and with a concussion.

"You know?" she whispers.

"I do now, yes."

Before she guesses what I'm planning to do, I've pulled the balaclava off her head. Her face is a patch of light in the darkness. Huge eyes, hair plastered to her scalp.

She quickly tugs the elastic band out of her hair and makes a new ponytail. As if that matters.

"Did you think it was funny?" I ask in a loud voice. "That I had no idea who you were and I just kept on babbling away? Did you tell Ziva and Elin and the others all about me?"

She shakes her head. "It wasn't like that."

"Yes, that's exactly what it was like! You sat there in my bedroom with that balaclava on your head, acting as if you didn't know a thing about me. As if I could tell you anything."

"I told you all kinds of things too, didn't I?"

"Just about that stupid robbery."

Alaska's standing between us. I watch her white head going to and fro: from Parker to me, from me to Parker—as if she's watching a tennis match.

But for once Parker is completely ignoring the beast.

"That robbery," she yells, "just happens to be the most important thing in my entire life!"

"Yes," I yell back. "I kind of realized that! And all men are evil and you know exactly how many of them are in prison. Seriously, how long are you going to go on whining about it?"

I brush the hair out of my eyes, but it blows straight back.

"Sometimes bad things happen. Deal with it! Your dad's shoulder is OK now, so get a high-tech alarm and if you're all still terrified in two months' time, then your mom and dad can sell the store and go and do something else instead. How hard can it be?"

"How hard can it be?" Her voice rings out across the field, high and shrill. "Those robbers are still walking around. And they've got a gun! You should be scared too. *Everyone* should be scared!"

I sigh. "Look around you, Barker. Everyone *is* scared. Or maybe they're not scared, just for a moment—but that's basically the same thing. Everyone knows the world is a scary place. So why are you allowed to be more scared than everyone else? Why are you allowed to whine about it constantly while the rest of us have to get on with living?"

She stands there, not saying a word.

Alaska whines. She nudges her nose against my leg, then Parker's hand. Then my hand, then Parker's leg.

"Just be glad," I say, "that you can be scared of a man with a gun. I have to be scared of myself. I could just keel over at any moment."

She takes a step back.

"I know," she says. "Poor, poor you, with your seizures and your key for the elevator and your brilliant stunt that you didn't pull off. But do you know something? Your epilepsy doesn't change anything. You're nothing special. You're still a mean little boy who picks on other kids on his very first day at school."

"Are you serious?! You're the one who started *barking* in the very first class."

She nods. "Yes, and thanks to you no one's ever going to forget that. You wanted to pull off a stunt, and that was exactly what you did. You came up with the dumbest nickname ever, and now everyone thinks you're cool. But you couldn't care less what they think about me."

The night is biting into my face. The wind's blowing harder and harder.

"Why should I care what they think of you?" I scream. "I've already got enough to worry about. Don't you get it? It's every man for himself!"

She stands there, very straight. Skinny, in her polo neck and her black pants.

"And that," she says quietly, "is exactly what those armed robbers thought too. *It's every man for himself.*"

I could thump her. I've never met anyone who's so good at exaggerating. And the entire time Alaska keeps pacing between the two of us. Whimpering quietly, her dark doggy eyes shining in the moonlight.

"Stop that whining," I shout. "Get a grip, beast." I grab her collar. "We're going home."

Parker's still holding the leash. No way am I going to ask that liar if I could please have the leash back. So I pull Alaska along by the collar.

"Let go of her," shrieks Parker. "You're hurting her!"

If you tried chopping a baby into bits and pieces, I imagine its mother would sound something like that.

"Alaska isn't a beast," she shouts. "She's the sweetest dog ever. And if you yank her collar like that, then she *feels* it. What do you think? That she exists to help you? That she's some kind of living alarm button?"

"Yes," I say. "That's exactly what I think. But she's dumber than an alarm button. You don't have to teach an alarm button anything. And it doesn't need treats."

Suddenly there are razors slicing through my leg. I slump forward and grab my shin with both hands.

Parker just kicked me. Really hard.

"Come on," she shouts at Alaska. "We're going!"

I've let the collar slip from my hand. Wagging her tail, Alaska runs to her old owner.

Parker doesn't even take the time to attach the leash. She just starts running.

"You don't deserve her," she yells at me. Her voice echoes across the dark field. "At least I love her!"

PARKER

Together with Alaska, I run through the night. We must have raced through the world together like this a thousand times before. She can run much faster than me, but she stays there beside me, galloping along, doing a couple of extra skips, tapping my hand with her nose, smiling with her black mouth.

I'm so angry that I can't think. *I hate him*—that's all. My entire head is packed full of *I hate him*s. I desperately hope that I don't twist my ankle, that I don't fall, that I get to my bike before him.

The balaclava is somewhere far away in the field, the wind is blowing through my hair, and I don't look back even once. And then I hear him calling.

"Alaaaska!"

She does a half spin in the air.

"Alaska, heeere!"

She glances at me, shakes her head so that her ears flap and then happily starts running back to her new owner. And he runs to her—as if they're two lovers who have forgotten all of their quarrels and are racing toward each other with open arms.

I stand there, panting. I'm cold as ice and hot as a volcano, all at the same time. Alaska was with me for eight months. Then she stayed with Yvonne for a month to learn all of her assistance-dog tricks. And now she's been with Sven for three months.

Just three months.

"Alaaaaaska!" I call, as loud as I can. The cold night fills my lungs. "Come on, girl!"

I see the white patch in the distance stop. For a moment, nothing happens. And then she heads back in my direction. Fur swinging, tail swishing.

"Alaska, here," Sven calls.

"No," I yell. "Here!"

"Seriously?" He's so close now that I can see his face. His hair is ruffled, and he's out of breath too. "You're trying to make her choose?"

I still have the leash in my hand, but it's no good to me without Alaska. She stops somewhere between us. She doesn't understand.

Of course I don't want to make her choose. That would be unbearably cruel. But at the same time, it's exactly what I want. I want to make her choose, because I love her more—and she knows that. I've been her owner for longer. I trained her so well that Yvonne saw immediately that Alaska could become an assistance dog. I don't call her a "beast," I give her as many hugs as she wants—and I never fall down on the ground, drooling and twitching.

"OK," I shout. "We'll let her choose. And whoever she chooses gets to keep her."

"Deal," says Sven.

I'm dizzy. It feels like this is the end. Alaska is going to choose, and then after that there's nothing. Just a black hole.

"How are we going to do this?" he shouts from a distance.

I once saw a duel in a film. Two men with guns stood back to back, and then they both walked twenty paces, turned around and shot. One hit the target. The other died.

"We'll walk away from each other," I say. "No calling out to her. We'll just walk. And then we'll see who she goes with."

"Fine by me."

"But you can't just walk back to your house. That wouldn't be fair."

"OK," he says. "I'll walk toward those flats over there in the distance. You can walk toward those trees."

Alaska has heard that we've stopped yelling at each other, so she's stopped worrying for now. She's sniffing the ground, halfway between us.

"We'll start walking on three," says Sven.

I clasp the leash. "So we won't call out to her. We'll just walk without saying anything. Right?"

"And we'll see who she chooses."

"One..." calls Sven.

"Two," I say.

"Three!" we shout together.

We start walking at the same time. Our backs facing each other. So this really is a duel. I don't know what's better— walking slowly, so that I can stay near Alaska for longer, or running, and hoping that she'll gallop off with me.

My heart pounding, I walk across the deserted field. I keep looking back and almost stumble over a piece of wood. My hands are cold. I want to shout, but I don't do it. She's going to choose me anyway. She was over the moon when I came through the dark sliding doors. She hears the way Sven talks to her every day—she knows that he hates her.

And then I see that white patch moving in the distance.

In the darkness, I can't quite make out which way she's running at first. For a moment I think: *Maybe she's running to and fro, maybe she's not sure, maybe she's saying goodbye to him.*

But the white dot is getting smaller and smaller. She's not coming back.

Alaska has chosen Sven.

SVEN

On Saturday morning, everything is the same, but everything is different too.

I have another seizure, but I don't need to go to hospital. When it started, I was sitting on the floor with the beast. She was whining so frantically that I looked to see if something was wrong. A sprained doggy ankle or a thorn in one of those gray paw pads or a twisted tail—how should I know?

When I come round again, she's lying beside me, panting. What is it with dogs? Even when they're not out of breath, they pant.

Whenever I go crashing to the ground, the beast has to do two things: press the alarm button and come and lie beside me. As soon as I'm back to normal, she goes crazy with excitement. She knows her reward is coming: dog biscuits from the most securely sealed jar ever. The things reek—it's like someone disemboweled a cow and left it to ripen for three weeks.

*   *   *

But Yvonne says it's not about the biscuits.

It's about me being back. About the short circuit being over.

According to her, Alaska and I have a special radio connection. During a seizure, that connection is broken and *that* is what an assistance dog hates more than anything: an owner who doesn't react. Losing the signal.

Slowly I see the white head coming into focus.

Panting, pink tongue. Wet, black nose.

She looks at my face, and waits. For the signal to come back.

Waking up in an ambulance is a nightmare. I have no idea where I am, and I get into a panic. Sometimes I scream. Sometimes I lash out and try to pull the drip out of my arm.

But when the beast is lying next to me, I know everything's OK.

I go on looking at her and think about last night.

I still can't believe it.

She knows I have seizures. She knows she has to wear a dumb vest with me, that I'm in a foul mood a lot of the time, and that everything could go wrong at any moment.

And still she wants me to be her owner.

She chose me.

PARKER

All weekend I feel sick. Out there in the dark field I thought: *Alaska is going to choose, and then after that there's nothing. Just a black hole.* And I was right. The black hole is inside my stomach now.

For three nights, I almost had her back again. My hands had just remembered what it felt like to stroke her. And now I've messed it all up. She watched us both walking away: her old owner and her new one. And then she chose him.

While I'm on the computer looking at photos of all the golden retrievers on Earth, I think about something that happened two years ago. At my old school, there was this boy in my class whose mom and dad were always arguing. When we were about nine, they finally got divorced. But the arguments went on. About the house. About how they were going to divide up all their stuff. And about how to divide up the children. One day at school, he told us that his mom had yelled that *he* had to make the decision: did he want to live with his dad? Or with her?

I can still see his face. His head wasn't covered with white fur, the classroom wasn't dark, and he wasn't standing fifty feet away from me. I could see his expression perfectly.

So I know. What Alaska must have looked like in the field. When her head was looking one way and then the other, at Sven and then me. When she realized she had to choose.

On Sunday night I don't set the alarm clock for two in the morning. That's all over now. I've never felt this bad about spending an entire night in bed before. And I can't even sleep. *Lying awake in bed is restful too*—that's what my mom always used to say.

That was before she started taking sleeping pills.

On Monday morning, I'm sitting next to the poster of the Eiffel Tower in the rain again. As I sort everything in my pencil case by size order, from big to small, I'm not waiting for anyone. But when Sven walks into the classroom, I suddenly can't remember how to sit in a chair like a normal person. He walks past me and I can't help myself: I quickly check to see if he has any new Band-Aids or bandages.

Nothing. Even the bandage on his bruised hand has gone.

Before he sits down, he looks at me for two seconds. And then he completely ignores me. I do exactly the same. He says "*Bonjour, je m'appelle Sven*" to Benjamin; I say "*Ça va bien, merci*" to Claire. He doesn't call me Barker; I don't tell anyone that he feels like a boy on Mars; he doesn't say anything about the robbery. So this is how it's going to be from now on.

But at lunchtime, it all goes wrong for Sven.

He's sitting with Benjamin on a bench on one side of the hall. Elin and I are sitting in the window seat on the other side. My eyes are supposed to be looking at my sandwich—that's the idea. But every thirty seconds, they keep darting over to Sven.

So I see him fall.

His body stiffens and, with one shout, he falls like a plank on to the floor. That shout has immediately alerted the entire hall: *Something's wrong!* He lies there perfectly still, stretched out on the floor. And then he starts shaking.

Elin and I run toward him—and so does everyone else. Within a few seconds, there's a huge circle around him. Last week Sven had three small seizures, so his spooky laughter doesn't send us into a panic anymore.

But this is different.

He's breathing in gasps. His eyes have rolled back, and his arms and legs are shaking like mad. Once I accidentally zapped past a film of a man being tortured: they kept giving him electric shocks. And that's what Sven looks like now.

"There's blood coming out of his mouth!" shouts Benjamin.

I feel dizzy.

Sven's head bangs on the black-and-white tiles with every movement. *Just be glad*, he said on Friday night, *that you can be scared of a man with a gun. I have to be scared of myself.* As I look at the bloody froth on his lips, I understand what he meant. I desperately try to remember what the handout said, the one about epilepsy that he gave out on the first day.

"We need to put something under his head," I shout.

But no one's listening.

Teachers come running. Elin is crying, one boy's filming it with his cell phone, people are screaming, and at least three students are calling the emergency number, even though it said in the handout that you should only call them if the seizure lasts longer than five minutes. But if they weren't calling, I'd be doing it myself.

My hands shaking, I take off my sweater. I kneel down beside Sven. I act like I'm not scared and carefully slide the sweater under his banging head. Otherwise I don't touch him—you're not allowed to hold on to him during a seizure. You can't stop the shaking anyway—all you'd do is hurt him.

I know that, inside my head, this is going to become another movie for viewers over the age of forty. His rolled-back eyes aren't looking at anyone, and his face is twisted. This isn't Sven, I tell myself—this is just his convulsing body. His blood is dripping on to my sweater, but he can't feel any of this.

Can he?

The teachers make a wider circle, to give him space. Their voices sound nervous. *Look around you*, Sven yelled in the field. *Everyone is scared.* I sit in silence on the floor beside him. What I really want to do is to run away as quickly as possible, but this is what Alaska does: she stays with him. She sees him shaking, she hears him groaning, but she stays.

Finally the seizure is over.

Did it last three minutes? Seven? Fifteen? I have no idea. Sven is lying beside me, not moving. He's wheezing, and his body is limp and pale.

Blockmans kneels down next to us and looks at me. "We can move him on to his side now," he says quietly. "So that he doesn't choke."

Together, we carefully roll him over. Sven has touched my shoulder once—and now I'm touching his. Very briefly, I let my hand rest there. He groans, and his eyes are unfocused. But suddenly he wants to sit up.

"Keep calm," says Blockmans. "You had a seizure. It's OK. Just lie there for a moment."

But Sven really wants to sit up. I can see that he's confused. He has no idea where he is.

And then the circle of students opens up. Two ambulance men come through. Yellow-and-turquoise uniforms, medical equipment. They're towering above us. And they take over.

They check Sven's pulse, talk to Blockmans and then the two of them discuss the patient. I stand up and move to the back without saying anything. I see Sven's face. The confusion. His complete helplessness. He can't explain what's happening to him right now, so they get to decide everything. They don't think he's broken anything, and they can see that the blood is because he bit his tongue, but to be on the safe side they decide to take him in anyway.

And, also to be on the safe side, he has to go on a stretcher. He doesn't want to—he doesn't understand. I wish I felt brave enough to take his hand and tell him it's OK, and that he has to go to hospital now, but Alaska will be waiting when he gets home.

But he's furious with me. I fooled him with my balaclava, so now he thinks I'm just a massive fraud. When he was having his seizure, I made sure he didn't bash his head to pieces. But now he doesn't want anything to do with me.

I watch him being wheeled off on the stretcher. As soon as the school doors close, everyone around me starts chattering away. I don't say anything.

Slowly, I walk back to the window seat, where there's still half a cheese sandwich on top of my bag. I'm about to throw it away, but then I hear Sven's voice inside my head again. *Why are you allowed to be more scared than everyone else? Why are you allowed to whine about it constantly while the rest of us have to get on with living?*

So I finish my sandwich.

SVEN

I'm just back from the hospital when the video arrives.

I'm lying in bed, exhausted. My head aches and my muscles ache and my tongue is all fat and sore because I bit it again. At the beginning of a seizure, every muscle in your body goes stiff. If your tongue happens to be between your teeth, then it's bad luck. Seriously, the doctors gave my mom and dad a warning: never try to free his tongue with your fingers. You'll lose them.

It's Sol who sends the video.

He says he doesn't know if I'll want to see it, but it's going all around the school right now. Classes are sending it on their group chat. And it's jumping from class to class, via friends, brothers and sisters.

OK. If the whole school's seen something, then I want to see it too.

I open the video.

Instantly, I'm sorrier than I've ever been. About anything.

It's my seizure—a whole two minutes and thirty-five seconds long.

They filmed me while I was out of it.

Last spring, I stayed at an epilepsy center. They tested medication on me, examined me every day, and the psychologist was pretty OK. But they also filmed a major seizure. And they asked me: do you want to see it?

I didn't even need to think about it: nope.

I saw other kids having seizures at the center. So I know exactly what happens. What order it all happens in, how the blood and drool drips down your chin, how your eyes roll back, what kind of zombie noises you make.

Seriously, let me be on another planet, while I fall apart.

But there I am, lying on the black-and-white tiles.

Shaking, frothing, grunting.

I can see it. And the rest of the school has seen it too.

For the first time in ages, I start crying.

Just seeing myself lying there, with that crowd around me. Like a circus act.

Knowing that it's me. That I'm like *that*.

And also knowing that someone thought it was funny to film it and send it to the entire universe.

*   *   *

I have absolutely no doubts about it, not even for a second.
I'm never going back to that school again.

PARKER

I can see the video on Benjamin's phone. From a distance—he sits in the row in front of me. But I can tell what it is right away. The scene from a torture movie, about a boy on Mars getting electric shocks.

No.

Sven, having a seizure. And me sitting next to him. I'm in the video too—but I'm not moving, I'm not bleeding, I'm not making any noise.

Blockmans has just been called away from the classroom, so I take out my own phone. The girl who lives across the road from me sent me the same video three minutes ago. We used to do art classes together, and now she's in the second year.

Parker!!! Whaaat? Scary stuff! Is he in your class? The two of you are going viral! It's all over the school!!!

I stare at the film. It's in color, not in black and white like the pictures from the security camera. But otherwise it feels exactly the same: seeing something again, something you've already seen for real when you were petrified. And even though you're not petrified now, there's still nothing you can do.

You can't ever change a thing about it. You saw that someone was filming it on their phone, but it didn't get through to you. Now it's too late—you can't stand up and smash that phone on to the floor.

"He's not coming back," I hear Sol say.

"Seriously?" says Benjamin.

"He's leaving school. Just sent me a message."

I clutch my phone.

It doesn't matter, I tell myself. I'm not allowed to see Alaska again anyway. It'll be easier if Sven leaves school. If Alaska is never waiting in the playground again.

Blockmans comes back into the classroom. He has a very serious look on his face.

"Listen up, guys," he says.

We all fall silent.

"So Sven Beekman had a major seizure this morning. We knew it would happen one day, and we also knew that everyone would be scared the first time. But I just spoke to Sven's mom, and it appears that one of our students filmed the seizure."

I can see cell phones under a lot of the desks. Some of the screens are still silently playing the clip.

"We are, of course, going to find out who made the video," says Blockmans. "But first we want to make sure that it doesn't end up on the internet. I'd like all of you, right this instant, to delete the video." He motions at us to take out our phones. "Come on. Get your phones out. For once, it's allowed."

All of the phones come out on to the desks. Some of the class are seeing the seizure for the first time. They whisper to me that I'm in the video too. Excitedly, they ask if I was scared. And they look at my black sweater, which I've put on again because I was cold without it. You can't see the bloodstains anyway.

As I delete the video, I know for certain that it won't disappear. Even if every teacher makes every class delete every video, it will still exist. Some people have already sent it to their friends at other schools. That's just how it works—that's the world. A bomb could explode somewhere at any moment. And videos that you send to more than two people will always continue to exist.

I try to tell myself all of this without thinking about Sven, but it doesn't work. I put my hand up.

"Sir, can I go to the toilet? I've already deleted the video."

Blockmans can't tell anything from a black screen, but I hold my cell phone up anyway. He nods and, with my phone in my hand, I stand up. Quickly, I leave the classroom. Down the long hall, all the way to the empty stairwell. Making a group chat for the class was Ziva's first job as the class representative, so I have Sven's number.

I can hardly breathe as I listen to the phone ringing.

And then he answers.

"I don't want to talk," he says right away.

On the phone he sounds younger than thirteen.

"Are you out of hospital yet?" I ask.

He clears his throat. "Which part of 'I don't want to talk' don't you understand?"

"I'm in the video too," I say.

"Seriously? As if that…" He stops.

On the other end of the line, I can hear him breathing.

I wonder if he's in his bedroom—the room I know. I wonder if Alaska is with him.

"Sol says you're not coming back to school. Is it true?"

It's a while before he answers.

"Yes," he says.

"Because of the video?"

"Because I've had enough of Mars. I've had enough of being the outsider."

"But you can't just... What are you going to do?"

He sighs. "There are schools where everyone's like me. So I won't stand out. Ambulances and pills and seizures are just normal there."

I press the phone to my ear. I try to remember that he's just a mean little boy. That I'm Parker the Barker because of him, that he calls Alaska "beast" and that he pulls really hard on her collar.

"You think you're the only one," I say quietly, "but that's not true. Everyone is walking around on Mars. You said yourself that everyone is scared. Well, it's the same with being different. We're all different. I have to spend all day explaining how I breathe too. And still no one gets it."

I look up at the gray concrete steps. Empty stairs for people without a special key for the elevator.

"Within three days they'll be used to your seizures. That's the advantage of a planet full of wildly different people. There's always something new. Tomorrow some Fifth Year will put her boobs online and then no one will think your torture movie is that fascinating anymore."

"What?" he says. "My *torture* movie?"

It feels as if gravity ceases to exist for a moment.

"Well, um..."

"Is that what you're all calling it?"

I shake my head. "No, just me. I mean, I saw this horror film once and..."

I can't go on.

For three seconds, I can still hear him breathing on the other end of the line. And then he hangs up.

SVEN

I put a chair next to my closet, stand on the seat and grab the helmet.

Alaska comes running over. She looks up curiously. Her head at an angle, tail slowly wagging.

I brush my hair from my forehead, put on the helmet and fasten the strap under my chin.

Today two things have been rammed into my head and they're never going to leave it.

Two minutes and thirty-five seconds of video.

And three words. *Your torture movie.*

I see the images on a phone screen.

And when I think of those words, I'll always hear the voice of Balaclava Girl.

So that's how she sees me. As an actor in a horror film.

Not as Sven the champion swimmer. Not as the Sven who always won at ditch-jumping, not as the Sven who could easily skate ten miles.

*   *   *

And, as I'm finally beginning to realize, she's right. I'm not that boy anymore.

Everything that I was is gone.

A year ago, I had a pile of paper shoved into my hands: here, you're getting the role of the boy with epilepsy. These are your lines. You don't have that many to learn. After all, most of the time you'll be lying on the ground, grunting.

It's time to get used to it.

This is my life.

I have an assistance dog, a bedroom on the ground floor, an SOS bracelet on my wrist, a bottle of pills and a helmet.

I'm Sven and I'm in the epilepsy club.

PARKER

Sven's desk stays empty. On Tuesday, and on Wednesday too.

He needs to recover from his seizure, of course. He's waiting for us to forget the video and then he'll be back next week. That's got to be it. What kind of parents would be OK with their son changing schools after just a week? If we all started doing that, then I should have moved schools right after "Jingle Bells." Moms and dads always say that you need to stop and think about things. That you need to discuss them, and that it's important to sleep on stuff.

But it seems that Sven's parents are different.

On Thursday morning, Blockmans comes into our math class. He says Sven isn't coming back. Never again.

"He's looking for a school that's more suitable for him."

He doesn't say what kind of school that might be. And I don't say that I'd like to go looking for a life that's more suitable for me. A life without robbers, without allergic little brothers and without cell phones making videos.

The whole class signs a card for him. There's a gorilla on the front, with a bunch of colorful balloons. *Dear Sven*, it says inside. *Good luck at your new school!*

When the card gets to me, I hesitate. Ziva has put a heart

on the *i* in her name instead of a dot. When I write my name, I make the *a* into a paw print.

Then, after that, as we're sitting there in deathly silence, doing our sums, I can't seem to keep my pencil completely still. The same thing happened the first week after the robbery. The entire time, my whole body was trembling a bit.

I think back to that night when I raced through the gleaming streets to Sven and Alaska. For weeks, it had felt like my body was slowly crumbling. If it continued, I was going to be like my dad. Just empty packaging.

Now I can feel it again. The crumbling.

With everything I do, another piece falls into the black hole. Class without Sven. A school playground without Alaska. Another afternoon with my little brothers marching around, while my dad sits silently looking at the pictures from the security cameras.

It's Thursday, so it's late-night shopping. Since eight o'clock, I've been sitting at the computer, next to my dad. We're watching Mom and Erik tidying up the store. We see a customer come in and we both hold our breath. Then we see the customer leave—and we breathe out.

"You're thirty-nine," I say to my dad. "Are you going to stay sitting here forever?"

"Of course not." He goes on staring at the screen.

"How much longer then?"

He shakes his head. "I don't know, Parker."

"Do you regret having four kids?" I ask.

He quickly turns his head to look at me. "Why would you think that?"

"Well..." I shrug. "If the world is so dangerous that all you can do is sit at home, looking at the pictures from the security cameras... Then it actually seems pretty odd to have four kids. Because all those kids have to go outside every day. To school and to the supermarket and to judo and to recorder classes."

I see his face twitch, and I'm not even shocked. These past few weeks, I've seen him cry at least ten times. The first time was awful, and I wished I was somewhere in New Zealand, all huddled up deep under the bedcovers. By the tenth time, I just wished he'd stop.

"You can be the one with the knife," I hear Dex shouting in the kitchen. "And I'll be the one with the gun."

"I want to be the one with the gun!" screams Joey.

"No, Joey." Finn sounds like that teacher of his. Calm, reasonable. "You're the one who gets shot. That's fun too, isn't it?"

Dad and I are still looking at each other. Nothing is ever going to smooth out the creases in his face.

"I'll go," I say.

I get up and walk toward the kitchen. But then my dad clears his throat.

"Hey, Parker. During Easter vacation, there was that card game that you guys kept wanting to play," he says.

I stop.

"How about we play it now?" he asks.

"You know it's twenty-five to nine, don't you?"

We both look at the screen again. In black and white, my mom is cleaning the counter.

"Yes," says my dad. "I know." He stands up. "I want to play the game now. With my four kids."

SVEN

I'm never getting out of bed again.

Why would I? The next seizure is going to happen at some point, so I'm better off already lying down.

The alarm button is waiting beside me; Alaska is waiting at my feet. And I'm waiting too.

I've had enough of crashing to the ground and getting injured and throwing hot tea over myself and tumbling through a window and breaking my wrist. I've had enough of ambulances and hospitals.

I'm just going to lie here.

PARKER

On Friday, after school, I'm feeling brave. I'm going on another bad-guy hunt. It's too cold to sit on a wall doing nothing, so I start walking. Street after street after street. I come to a neighborhood I don't know very well, but that doesn't matter. Thieves can be anywhere.

As I walk along a gray sidewalk past gray houses, I wonder what Sven and Alaska are doing now. How long will this go on? How long will they be walking invisibly beside me with everything that I do?

It's four o'clock. Now he's feeding her.

Now they're going for a walk.

Now he's giving her a brush.

Now they're going to sleep.

The past few days, whenever missing her got too bad, I went online and read websites about assistance dogs. So I could still kind of feel close to Alaska. So I could imagine what her days are like now.

Now she's practicing with the alarm button.

Now she's got some time off and she's running through the wood without her vest on.

Now she's the only dog allowed in the supermarket.

*   *   *

And then, suddenly, I see two black sneakers with red flames on the sides of the soles.

I stop breathing.

The sneakers are walking along the other side of the narrow street—and everything about them is right. The messy way they're laced up. The way the soles are a bit worn out. And both of the tongues are just a little too far to the right.

I take my phone out of my bag and stand there. As I turn off the sound with a shaking finger, the man with the flaming shoes walks on, as calm as anything. If I don't go after him right now, I'm going to lose him.

I'm dizzy.

So dizzy that I think I'm going to black out for a moment—but I start walking again anyway. Back to where I came from. Following him. He's wearing gray sweatpants and a black jacket. His hair is short and there are spots on the back of his neck. I can't see his face.

All that time I've never imagined what I'd do if I actually found him. I went out on my bad-guy hunts. Looking for some cartoon character in black-and-white striped pajamas. But now here we are, the bad guy and me, all alone in a silent street. If I call the police, he'll hear me speaking. If I stop to use the phone, I'll lose him.

I feel just like I did during the robbery: I can't think properly. But I have absolutely no doubt about the shoes. Not for a second. Hidden behind the coats at the back of the store, I just stared at his feet. The picture is burnt into my brain. And the picture is right. There, on the other side of the street—it's him.

He goes around the corner.

I cross the road, close my eyes for a moment and then follow him.

Six weeks ago, that man had a shiny gun in his hand. Not a toy gun, a real one. I have no idea if it's under his jacket now. Do robbers always take their guns with them, just in case? The way other people are glued to their phones and fall apart if they lose their signal for a second?

Maybe that's how it feels with a gun: like you've always got a signal wherever you go. Without having to pay for it.

My stomach hurts; my heart's thumping loud enough to deafen me. Whatever I do, I'm not going to send my mom and dad a message. If they know I'm here on my own, following the man with the gun, they'll be so angry.

I clasp my fingers around my telephone. The screen comes to life, and I stare at the photo of Alaska. And suddenly I know what I need to do. My brain's working again. It's like finally keying in the right password after you've tried a bunch of wrong ones.

I start typing.

Can see robber!!! And his shoes!
What shd i do???

I press *Send.* And quickly add my location.

There's no stopping the videos inside my head now. I see my mom standing behind the counter, her face as white as chalk. I see my dad diving for the alarm button, and I hear the gun go off. The man walking ahead of me, past the window boxes full of geraniums, was the one who pulled the trigger.

I see the puddle of blood on the floor, after they took my dad to hospital with screaming sirens.

And then I feel the phone vibrating in my hand. It's Sven's reply.

Call the police!
Make sure he doesn't see you!!!

> *Can't call polite he'll hear*
> *Police*

Want me to call them?

> *Yes!!!*

OK
BRB
Be careful!!!

SVEN

I'm sitting up in bed. I've never called the emergency number before.

All those times that people called the number for me, I was out of it. I was shaking away on the floor while they keyed in the numbers, while they waited for someone to answer.

"Emergency services. Operator speaking," says a man's voice. "Which service do you require? Police, fire brigade or ambulance?"

Ambulance, I almost say. But I'm not having a seizure this time.

"Police," I say.

As they're putting me through, I look at Alaska. I'm still lying in bed—this is day four. All that time, absolutely nothing has gone wrong. It's like falling stars. If you keep looking, nothing ever falls.

"Police," says a woman's voice. "What's your emergency?"

"Hi, my name's Sven," I say quickly. "You have to arrest someone. This summer there was a robbery at Montijn Photographic Supplies. And now Parker, that's their daughter—the owners of the store, I mean..."

I take a deep breath.

"Parker has just tracked down one of the robbers. She recognized his shoes. He was wearing a balaclava—during the robbery, I mean—so she didn't see his face. But he had sneakers with red flashes of lightning on the sides of the soles. Or flames—I can't remember. But anyway, she was just following him, like, two minutes ago, on Roerstraat. You have to send the police right away!"

"Is Parker injured?" asks the woman on the other end of the line.

"No. Not yet..."

"And she's following a man she suspects of having committed a robbery?"

"Yes."

"But she's not being threatened?"

"No."

"And she's never seen the robber's face, but the man she's following is wearing the same sort of shoes as the man who committed the robbery?"

"Yes, I already told you that! Black sneakers with red on the soles."

"This emergency number," says the woman calmly, "is for emergencies. If you have any tips for the police, you can call the national police hotline."

"But Parker is going after the man right now. On her own!"

"Then she should stop right away. She must not put herself in danger. And she can call the hotline. This emergency number is not for children who are playing detective."

"Oh, really?" I yell. "It's you lot who are making such a mess of the world. And when Parker recognizes a robber, it's suddenly supposed to be her fault that she's in danger?"

"I can assure you," the woman says so calmly that I could thump her, "that the police take every tip seriously. But this number is intended only for emergencies. And right now you're blocking the line for a real emergency."

She hangs up.

Every stupid, lame seizure I have, they come racing up with their sirens wailing, but when Parker sees the man who shot her dad, it's not an emergency.

Another message comes in.
  Sven!!!
  Where are they?

I clench my fists.

I was planning never to get out of bed again. And *if* I ever went outside, it would only be with someone else. Exactly the way you're supposed to do things when you're in the epilepsy club.

I was also planning never to say another word to Parker. But that was last week—a millennium ago. An incredibly dull millennium ago.

The emergency services don't get it, but I do. As soon

as that man realizes he's being followed, it *will* become an emergency.

Parker sends me her new location and I stare at the map. If I walk, it'll take me at least half an hour to get there. Way too long.

God, this is crazy.

I'm not allowed to use my bike. Absolutely, definitely not. My bike moved house with us, but I haven't been on it for months.

It's obvious what I should do. I need to phone my mom. She's gone to the supermarket, but if I call she'll come straight home. Then we can both get in the car and go to Parker.

I can see it in HD: my mom's worried face, her shrill voice, the two of us together in the car—and I suddenly find myself throwing back the quilt. I get out of bed and start pulling on my clothes, because now I can see *everything*. The rest of my entire rotten life if I stay lying here now.

Imagine if all you did all day was wait for seizures.

I'm afraid of dying—of course I am. But lying in bed, year after year after year—that's worse than being dead. That's worse than concussions and injuries.

*   *   *

I put Alaska's yellow vest on her, and she immediately starts wagging her tail in delight. Every assistance dog's nightmare is that your owner is a coward who stays in bed for the rest of his life.

I hesitate for a moment before putting on the helmet. If I do go crashing off my bike, I'll be better off with a head made of plastic.

My bike's right at the back of the shed. I hate it that my hands are shaking. That I'm scared of *cycling*.

And all that time, Parker's been following the robber. I hope he hasn't spotted her. How many streets can you trail someone for before they notice something's up?

She sends her location again and I answer that help will be there in ten minutes. She doesn't need to know that she'll be waiting for an epileptic kid and his assistance dog.

So now I'm going out on my bike, with Alaska beside me. That's one thing the beast hasn't learned how to do. When you're the assistance dog of a loser who's not allowed to use his bike, you don't need to learn much about traffic. She can cross the road, from one sidewalk to the other. But racing along beside a bike? Nope, she's never done that before.

And yet, somehow, she can do it anyway.

Balaclava Girl was right: Alaska is a circus dog. Half of the time she's almost pulling me over—she's going too fast or too slow and she keeps nearly wagging her tail in between the spokes—but we're getting there.

Seriously, I'd forgotten what it felt like. The wind in your face. Legs pedaling, lungs panting. Like you're *living*.

People are staring at me, with my helmet and my assistance dog, but right now I couldn't care less.

Parker sends her location again. I'm almost there. I clench my jaw.

Please, I think. *Not a seizure. Not now.*

I'm going too fast, the tarmac's flying by, cars are racing past us—if I have a short circuit now, it's not going to end well.

For me. For Alaska. Or for Parker. Is crazy Balaclava Girl still following that criminal? Where on earth is he going?

And then I see her coming around the corner. Alaska spots her at exactly the same moment. She does her high-pitched baby bark and at the same time I feel a huge tug on the leash. I try to keep hold of it, but then I remember the girl I used to live next door to. She once went for a walk with a massive dog. The dog saw a cat, went after it and, for twenty yards, the girl didn't let go of the leash. I saw her knees and hands and arms afterward. All covered in blood.

Alaska races over to Parker, ears flapping as if she's acting in an advert about happy dogs, dragging the leash behind her.

I thought Parker would be mad when she saw us. She wanted the police. But her face lights up when she looks at us. I get off my bike and push it on to the sidewalk.

"You two have come as well!" she whispers, as Alaska jumps up at her and licks her right in the face.

"When are the police going to get here?" Parker grabs the leash and starts walking again.

In the distance, I can see just one man.

"Is that him?" I ask quietly.

She nods. "When are the police getting here? Should I tell them where we are again?"

I shake my head. "They're not coming."

"What?"

"I called the emergency number, but they won't come. They say this isn't an emergency situation."

She doesn't reply. Looking very pale, she walks beside Alaska. Every inch of her body is screaming *emergency situation*.

We come to a busier part of town. I park my bike against a lamp post and take the leash back from Parker, to complete the picture: boy with helmet and assistance dog. Pale, silent girl without dog.

We need to get closer to the robber now, or we'll lose him. We don't dare to speak, scared that he'll hear us.

God, this is useless.

How long are we going to keep it up? Soon the guy's going to get on a scooter and he'll be gone. And then we won't have anything. No proof at all. Don't think that's going to impress them much at the national police hotline.

But suddenly I have an idea.

"Take a photo of Alaska and me," I whisper. "With the rest of the street in it too. Nice, eh, with all these people around..."

She looks at me, and I can see she understands.

PARKER

I thought I was never going to see Sven and Alaska again. And now they're walking beside me, as if we belong together. The robber is on the phone. I can see his hand waving about, his head nodding. With every step, he's getting closer to the town center. To the shops. To Montijn Photographic Supplies.

I try not to look at the blue helmet on Sven's head. I saw it on his bedroom floor that very first night. I thought it was an ice-hockey helmet. Or for mountain climbing or something. But Sven could fall at any moment, of course.

"Go on. Take the photo," he whispers.

My cell phone is shaking in my hand. If I'm not careful, I'm going to drop it, and it'll smash into pieces. The idea is simple: take a photo with the robber in it too. So that I can go to the police station and say: "Look, this is him. You didn't believe me, but this is the man who shot my dad."

"But if I take a photo now," I whisper, "all you'll see is the back of his head. How can..."

The robber stops using his phone, and I instantly lose the power of speech. Alaska is walking between us, with a serious expression on her face. She looks different now that she's wearing her assistance-dog vest. She's at work, and she knows it.

I wonder if she remembers that night out in the field. Can her doggy mind think back to things that happened a week ago? Does she remember that I made her choose?

And then I feel Sven's arm around my shoulder. His mouth is suddenly very close to my ear.

"I've got a plan."

I don't say anything. As I wait for him to tell me, I think again about how different it feels: being touched by a dog, and by a boy.

"Make sure you're ready with your phone," he says quietly. "I'm going to start screaming, and that guy will obviously turn around to have a look. And then you can take a photo."

I can feel his breath on my cheek. The edge of his helmet against my head.

"But we're not supposed to be drawing attention to ourselves," I whisper.

"I'm me, remember? I can't help attracting attention. It's what I do."

If I turned my face right now, we'd bump noses. He lets go of me, and I quickly put my phone in camera mode. Sven stands in front of me, but so that I can still see the robber. And then he starts barking.

"Jingle Bells"—at the top of his voice.

The man looks around. Alaska goes crazy and I take as many photos as I can, but I have no idea how they're going to come out. And then Sven shuts up.

The whole world is staring at us. Everyone—except for the robber. He's already hurrying on.

I swipe through the photos. "They're blurred."

"Then we'll just do it again," says Sven.

Quickly, we start walking. I'm out of breath. Sven is wearing a helmet, Alaska is in her harness, but otherwise they're the boy and dog I already know. Alaska is walking nicely on her leash, and Sven is humming a Christmas tune.

I know that all kinds of things could happen at any moment. Bombs could explode, the robber could start shooting, the world could come to an end. But with Sven and Alaska there, it feels different. I've seen the two of them forever and ever in that dark bedroom and somehow it feels as if the room is still here. As if we have walls around us.

But then Alaska stops walking nicely on the leash. She looks at Sven and begins to whine. She nudges his leg with her nose.

"Stop it, beast," he says, but Alaska doesn't listen. She tugs on the leash and walks in front of his feet, so that he nearly trips over her. She stares at him and gives a short bark. And then another one.

"What does she want?" I ask. "She never used to do that with me."

"She's just weird." He shrugs. "That morning after the storm she did the same thing. And on Saturday morning too. It's normal. She just does that sometimes."

I look at Alaska and I am certain that this is not "normal." In the eight months she lived with us, she never looked that worried. She never nudged away at anyone's leg like that, as if something terrible was about to happen.

Then I remember something I read online. Some assistance dogs can predict seizures. They see the epileptic fit coming, before you have any idea as a human that you're about to start shaking. Predicting seizures isn't something you can teach a dog, because people don't understand how it works. And most assistance dogs never get the hang of it. But yeah, some of them do.

"Saturday morning?" I say quickly. "When she did that... Did you have a major seizure afterward?"

He nods. "But I was already sitting next to her on the floor, so I didn't fall. I didn't get hurt."

"Lie down," I say.

"What?" He stares at me in surprise.

"You're going to have a seizure. That's what Alaska's trying to tell us. Lie down, or you'll hurt yourself when you fall."

"That's crazy," he says. "We have to follow that guy, remember? We need to take more photos."

We're still walking. Alaska keeps whining and nudging. And Sven could fall to the ground at any moment. I clench my fists. Finally I've found the robber. If I let him go now without getting any good pictures, then I'll be just as scared tomorrow. Or even more scared, because now I know that he's still here. In my town.

But I can't leave Sven behind. I need to be with him when the shaking starts. It's that simple.

"Lie down," I say. "Now!"

"That's crazy," he says again. "Not even doctors can predict when I'm going to crash. What are you trying to say? That the beast can do magic? That she's psychic or something?"

I look at Alaska. I know her better than anyone in the world. She's trying to tell us something—there's absolutely no doubt about it.

"If I've got it wrong," I say, "then you can laugh at me later. But first—lie down. There, on the grass."

If I hadn't seen that seizure on Monday, I wouldn't dare to do this. But if he's about to turn into a plank, then he needs to lie down. I drag him by his sleeve to a patch of grass around a statue. Then I sit and pull him down with me. Alaska lies beside him and starts licking his hand.

He frowns. "She does that whenever I have a seizure too."

Everything inside my body is trembling now. I could almost imagine that I can feel it coming too. But humans can't predict when someone's about to have an epileptic seizure. Not even machines in hospitals can do it. Only dogs.

"This grass is wet," says Sven. "Seriously, nothing's going to happen."

"Do you want me to call an ambulance when it starts?" I ask. My hand is stroking Alaska's soft back. She's still anxious.

"No. Please don't." He refuses to lie down. But sitting on the grass will work too, I think. I hope.

"You should only call an ambulance if the shaking's been going on for five minutes. Seriously. I've had enough of hospitals. And ambulances. You can call my mom though—you know, if I do crash."

He gives me his phone and I look around. The robber is long gone. My photographs of him are blurred and the emergency number won't listen to us, so following him all that way was completely pointless. And now I'm sitting here next to a furious Sven, and nothing's happening.

He looks at me, but I don't look back.

SVEN

She's staring at the street that the robber disappeared into, as she sits there beside me on the soaking wet grass.

Her face is still pale, but both her cheeks are flushed bright red.

Balaclava Girl, beside me on the grass.

I came to help her. And now we're sitting here waiting for a seizure that's not going to happen.

I'm an idiot in a helmet, I tell myself. A boy sitting next to an assistance dog on a damp patch of grass, waiting for a star to fall.

Yet somehow, I don't feel like an alien right now.

When my mom and dad look at me—yes, then I'm sick. In an ambulance, with doctors, at the epilepsy center, with my key for the elevator, completely out of it in a new class at school—yup, then too.

But Parker and Alaska, Balaclava Girl and the beast...

There's something weird going on with those two.
I don't have to explain anything to them.
They know my planet. They're u s e d   t o   m...

PARKER

The moment he stiffens, I feel my own body go stiff too. He lies there on the grass for a second, perfectly still, and then he starts shaking. For the past few minutes, I've been rehearsing inside my head what I need to do now. That's why I can do it. I don't need to think. I just do it.

First I turn on the timer on my phone.

Sven's wearing a helmet, so I don't need to put anything under his head this time.

I don't look at his eyes rolling back. I don't want to listen to his gasping breath. Alaska is whimpering. Her dark eyes are huge, and there's a frown on her doggy face.

"He can't feel anything," I whisper to her. "It's OK."

He's frothing at the mouth again, but this time it's not red.

I had it all planned, all except for the people. All those grown-ups who are coming up to interfere.

"He's having an epileptic fit," I keep saying. "It'll be over soon. It happens to him all the time. Really, there's no need for anyone to call an ambulance."

I see a man taking out his phone anyway.

"No!" I shout. "Don't call them! He doesn't need a doctor. I'll call his mom—that's enough."

So this is what it's like. Walking around on Mars. New people all the time, people who don't understand. Who stick their noses in without any idea what's going on.

I want to cry, but there's no time for that.

In Sven's telephone, there's a shortcut to *Mom cell*. She answers right away.

"Sven! Is everything OK?"

"It's not Sven," I say quickly. "This is Parker. Um, I'm a friend of Sven's. We were taking Alaska for a walk and he had a fit. A big one. Can you come and fetch us?"

"Oh, God..." She takes a deep breath. "OK, where are you? Is he injured? Does he need an ambulance?"

I can hear from her voice that she's like Alaska: she's done this plenty of times before. She wants to whimper, but she does exactly what needs to be done. As I'm talking to her, I see that Sven has stopped shaking. All the busybodies who were still standing around, who didn't like it one bit that we didn't need them, start to drift away.

Alaska keeps licking Sven's hand. I look at his pale face and feel like I've just survived an earthquake. Last time, I rolled him on to his side with Blockmans, but I can do it on my own too. The handouts call it the "recovery position." So that he won't choke on his own spit.

"You haven't hurt yourself," I whisper to him. I don't know if he can hear me yet. "You were out for less than three minutes, and the seizure's over now. Your mom's on her way."

Alaska keeps on licking away, and I keep on talking. There are no screaming sirens, and no one straps him into a stretcher. And as I'm talking, I look at Alaska as if I'm seeing her for the very first time. I thought I knew her inside out. Every fold in her fur, every spark in her brain, every trick she can do. But there's more.

She knew Sven was going to have a fit. She warned him. If only I understood how she can see it coming. Does she listen extra hard? Does she feel something? Can she smell a seizure? But no one knows the answer.

Sven starts coughing. I rest a hand on his shoulder, but then take it away.

"What?" he croaks. Then he frowns. "My back's wet."

I almost laugh, but I stop myself. He's still not quite awake.

"You're lying on the grass," I say. "Don't worry. Your back will dry out."

A red car drives up on to the sidewalk and the driver's door flies open. The blond woman who was waiting in the playground with Alaska, that first day, jumps out of the car.

"Sven!" She runs over to him. "Are you OK?"

"My back's wet," he says angrily.

I can see that he still hasn't realized what's going on.

His mom looks at me. "I'm so glad you called me. What was your name again?"

"Parker," I say. And then I have to say it. "Alaska saw the fit coming! She warned us, and that's why Sven didn't fall."

"Really?" his mom says. "Are you sure?"

Before I can reply, Sven butts in. "I don't get why we're still sitting here. This grass is soaking wet!"

His mom nods. "Come on. Let's go home. Parker, can I give you a lift?"

I hesitate. There's nothing I'd like more than to go straight home in a car. But I shake my head.

"I can't go home yet. There's something I need to do."

SVEN

The mist has gone. I'm back again.

I'm not sitting in the front of the car next to my mom, but in the back seat. Alaska is lying beside me.

When I look at her, I don't see a beast but a person. A person with a furry face and triangular eyes. Like holes cut into a snow-white balaclava.

Alaska looks back at me, and I know that she doesn't see a vague blob. She doesn't see an alien, or my illness. She sees *me*.

Whoa, so I guess Yvonne was right.

Alaska and I have a radio connection. A connection that's better than anything a human could come up with. Studying for ten years to be a doctor, MRI scanners, ultrasound machines, EEGs—nothing beats a hairy monster.

When you make an online call, they sometimes ask how many stars you'd give the connection.

Well, Alaska?

Seriously?

More stars than there are in the universe.

I look at the long whiskers sticking out of her snout like antennae. At her soft floppy ears and her shiny nose.

And then I put my arms around her.

Hey, I'm just as bonkers as Balaclava Girl. What's the point of loving someone you can't play computer games with, or go ice skating with?

But yeah, I never thought she'd learn how to do it.

I knew some assistance dogs could see a fit coming. And I knew that it changed everything for their owners. No more surprises, no more suddenly crashing to the ground, no concussions or arterial bleeding.

I've read about those super-teams of dogs and their owners in the magazine about assistance dogs. Iris and Bieke. Corrie and Cisko. Melanie and Snow. They made me furious, because I knew I'd never belong to a super-team like that. As if someone could ever see the rotten short circuit in my head coming, when I didn't have a clue myself.

But now here we are. Right here in the back seat.

Sven and Alaska. The new super-team.

PARKER

I try to act like Sven is still having a seizure. Then I knew exactly what I needed to do. There was an earthquake going on right next to me, but Alaska and I didn't panic. We did what we had to do.

Without a dog and without a helmet, I walk along the shopping street. My hands in my pockets, as if I've got a gun and I'm the only one who knows about it. My hair in the cold wind, my jaw clenched. In one straight line, I head for Montijn Photographic Supplies.

I open the door and step through. For the very first time, I go back into the store. And then I stop. It's not just my mom behind the counter—my dad's there too. They're sitting there, next to each other. Above their heads is the brightly colored poster: *Armed robbery! Always take CARE!* Unseen, beneath the counter, the red alarm button waits.

I start crying.

They both come running.

"Sweetheart, what is it?" My mom puts her arms around me without waiting for an answer. The way that Alaska starts licking when Sven's still confused.

"I saw him!" I cry into the darkness of her hug. "The robber! The man with the gun!"

I had no idea my dad would be here too. I thought he was still at home watching security images. I was going to tell my mom the whole story first, and then we could decide together if Dad needed to know. But now they're getting to hear the whole story together. About me recognizing the sneakers with the red flames. About Sven calling the police for me, and the police refusing to come. And about Sven coming instead—Sven with Alaska.

Yes, with Alaska. I tell them that I've seen her again. That she's the best assistance dog in the world. We had no idea what an amazing super-dog we had living with us for eight months.

"I tried to take some photos..." My hands shaking, I swipe through the blurry pictures. "But then Sven had an epileptic seizure and we let the robber get away." I look at my mom. "So he's still walking around here somewhere. About half an hour ago, he was heading in this direction. He might even have walked past the store."

I don't dare look at my dad. He's taken the telephone from my hands and keeps swiping through the blurred photos.

"Why didn't you call me?" my mom asks. Her face is very serious. "Or send a message, if you couldn't phone?"

I don't reply.

I wanted to be brave. My mom and dad have seen enough films for viewers over the age of forty. I wanted to solve the problem myself, but it backfired. So now we know that the man with the unknown face and the black sneakers is still out there, somewhere nearby. You can rob a store and shoot someone and then calmly go out for a bit of a walk around town.

"That guy..." My dad is thinking. "You said he had a cell phone, didn't you? And the phone was on? You saw him using it?"

I nod and wipe my nose on the back of my hand.

"And your phone was on the entire time too?"

I nod again.

"And how long were you near him? Any idea?"

"At least twenty minutes. Sometimes he stopped and stood there for a bit. And then he started walking again."

I look at my dad's face. Since the robbery, his eyes have been dull. But there's a little something twinkling away in them now.

"We're going straight to the police station. Right now," he says. He still has my phone in his hand. "Your phone was on the entire time, so your location will have been tracked. If they compare those details with the details of all the other cell phones in the area, then maybe they can work out which phone you were following all that time."

Mom and I stare at him. It's him: my dad from before. He always had ideas, he built his own cameras, and when we all watched a movie together, he knew who the bad guy was within ten minutes.

Inside the police station, everything is blue and white. There are officers walking around here who know what it feels like to have a gun on your hip at all times, and it smells of coffee, and they have prison cells on the other side of the building. While we're waiting for the detective, I listen to see if I can hear any criminals banging on the walls of their cells.

In my head, I'm rehearsing what I'm about to tell them. About the shoes. About following him. And about the phones. The police obviously don't need to hear all about Sven and Alaska, but it's impossible to erase the images from my mind. I can still feel Sven's arm around my shoulders. I can hear his words in my ear.

I'm me, remember? I can't help attracting attention. It's what I do.

He thinks he's the weirdest weirdo of all. And I guess it's not surprising. That very first day at school, there was no brilliant stunt, just spooky laughter. And a week later, half the town saw his torture movie. I told him that we're all weird. That everyone would forget about his fit before long. But I was wrong, because no one's sending any new clips around. Sven is still the only alien in the entire school.

Suddenly I have a plan.

I have no idea if it's going to work, and I don't know if it'll make any difference to Sven. But I can't forget it: he came to help me. Him and Alaska. He knew I was going after a criminal, the emergency people wouldn't listen, he wasn't actually supposed to use his bike at all, and we'd fallen out. But still he came.

I glance to the side. My dad is sitting next to me, with a very straight back. If you didn't know, you wouldn't be able to tell which shoulder had a bullet in it.

Without saying anything, I pick up my phone and look for Benjamin's number. I wish I'd come up with a one-person plan, something I could do all alone. But that's impossible. Everyone in 1B, all the kids who have been laughing at me for two weeks now—all of them have to help.

I've never spoken a word to Benjamin and until three minutes ago I wasn't planning to either. But everyone thinks he's funny, and he's friends with Sven. If I want to get my class to do something, I'd better start with Benjamin.

Hi, I type. My fingers hesitate. He's obviously going to be quite surprised that I'm suddenly talking to him. *Can I ask you something?*

I sit there, staring at the screen. Benjamin comes online almost immediately.

Hey, Barker!

The silver bullet. My whole class is full of annoying little brats. What I'd really like to do is smash my phone on to the floor, but I don't do that. If I go ahead with my plan, they're going to call me Barker even more. That's exactly my point: that we're all barking mad. Each and every one of us.

Benjamin starts typing again.

Lolz sorry ☺ But is it true tho??
That you were born in a park?

I bite my lip.

> *No*
> *At home*
> *But my mom and dad thought*
> *Bed was a boring name*

He's quiet for a moment. And then:

Ha ha ha
Ha ha

Mine thought Hospital sucked too
So...what's up?

> *Wanted to ask you something*
> *It's about Sven*

Yeah?

> *Got a plan*
> *But I can't do it on my own...*

SVEN

We're eating quinoa salad with roasted pumpkin. Alaska's having steak.

My mom went specially to the butcher's to get the steak for her. While she was out, I gave the beast a brush.

Cell phones are strictly forbidden at the table, but suddenly my dad's phone makes an extra-important sound. While he's checking his message, I take a quick look at my screen too.

There's a new message in the 1B group chat.

It's not my class anymore, but Ziva hasn't removed me from the group yet. And I haven't left it. I've already paused five times with my thumb hovering over *Leave group*. But pressing those words would feel even worse than leaving school.

I open the message. A video—and under it in massive letters: *1B IS THE COOLEST CLASS IN THE SCHOOL! On Monday you met Sven. Now meet Parker! Check it out and send it on!!!*

I click on the video and almost choke on a bit of pumpkin.

It's Parker. At the computer, with a fluffy, snow-white puppy on her lap. There's a Christmas tree behind her, and "Jingle Bells" is ringing through the room.

Parker and the puppy are barking along to the song. They're going too fast half the time, making up extra notes as they go, but if anyone ever wondered what the happiest puppy in the world looks like—well, that's it, right there.

Last week I'd have just got mad and clicked it shut. No way I'd have wanted to see that second-hand beast having a fun singalong with her old owner.

But now Alaska is *my* dog. The only one who sees my seizures coming. And yes, it's lame—but I'm melting at the sight of that little mutt on the screen.

Seriously, so that's what Alaska looked like as a baby? The other half of my super-team, with a tiny little snout and snow-white fluff instead of fur.

I turn up the sound on my phone as loud as it will go.

"We're eating!" says my mom indignantly.

But then she sees Alaska. The real one, not the ball of cotton wool on my screen. The grown-up beast comes dancing up, still licking her lips after the steak. She nudges my phone with her nose and starts barking along.

I play the video again and look at the baby on the screen and then at the big assistance dog beside me.

And yes, I look at Parker a bit too.

I only know her as Balaclava Girl. With rings under her eyes and nervous hands. But in the video she's wearing a red sweater with reindeer on it. And her face is glowing. Just like this afternoon, when she saw Alaska and me.

"That's Parker!" my mom exclaims. She leans over my shoulder. "And is that...Alaska?"

Silently, I go on staring at the video. Over and over again.

The second video comes in when I'm sitting in front of the television.

1B IS STILL THE COOLEST CLASS IN THE SCHOOL. Benjamin is at least as nuts as Sven and Parker. Check it out and send it on!!!

A sunny lawn full of daisies. Benjamin is half the size that he is now and he's wearing a colander on his head. He's dancing around a big circle of cuddly toys. Each of the toys has a cup of tea and a prettily decorated slice of cake.

"Look, Mommy," Benjamin shouts into the camera. "Teresa's already finished her tea! Now we're going to have presents. And then we're all going to sing for Crockie!"

My head still feels heavy from the seizure, and my muscles are stiff. But I can't help it: I burst out laughing.

The third video comes in a quarter of an hour later. Claire's playing a game and she's swearing so much that I turn off the sound on my phone super quick.

Three minutes later, it's Ziva in front of a mirror. She's got a mega-zit on her forehead and she's shrieking hysterically that there's no way she's going to school like that.

The fifth one is Sol, dressed from head to toe in orange, like the Dutch national soccer team. He's sobbing in front of the TV, while someone in the background is laughing his head off.

"Dude," a voice yells, "you've just got to accept it. They suck!"

Sol starts crying even louder.

They mention my name with every clip that's posted, like I'm still in 1B. Like I still belong.

I read all of the comments, but I don't write anything myself.

While I'm waiting for more videos to arrive, I go back and watch Parker's. I play it without any sound. I look at her face without the balaclava. Her eyes, her nose, her mouth.

This afternoon we nearly caught that robber. But when Alaska started whining, Parker didn't hesitate for a second. She let the man with flames on his shoes walk away. And she stayed with me.

If Balaclava Girl were a dog, I'd give her ten steaks.

PARKER

The videos are coming in faster and faster. I had no idea my class was so crazy. I'm sitting on the floor in the living room, with my phone plugged into the socket. After every video, we all leave comments, of course. But this time the idea is not to be cool and normal and just right. Today, all of 1B is dancing around on Mars.

Sven is the only one in the class who hasn't reacted yet. Does he think this is the lamest idea ever, a really bad stunt? Or does he just not care what we do anymore?

"Everything OK down there on the floor?" asks my mom.

"Yes..." I look at my mom and dad, and for the first time in a lot of weeks, a bit of me doesn't crumble away.

"Everything OK up there on the sofa?" I ask.

They nod at the same time. The television is off, but they're still sitting there together. They're drinking wine and they've said we can go to bed as late as we want to. As long as we stop marching around and giving orders. From today, marching is no longer part of our upbringing. I abandon my phone for a bit and go and fetch more chips. My brothers have been hiding under the kitchen table for at least an hour. They're having a meeting—in whispers.

"...buried in the yard," I hear Finn say.

"The bathroom is our new base," whispers Dex.

"And all of the toilet rolls are bombs," Joey shouts excitedly.

I know what's going on down there—it's the beginning of a secret resistance army. I push the rest of the bag of chips under the table with my foot, pretend I didn't hear anything, and head back to the living room.

This evening at the police station, my dad wasn't a crumpled-up ball of paper. He sat there with a serious expression on his face and explained to the detective that I'd followed the suspect for at least twenty minutes. Which meant our phones had also been close to each other for at least twenty minutes. And therefore he suspected that the police should be able to track down the man.

I held my breath when the detective didn't answer for ages.

"We can't just request information about cell-phone locations," he said finally. "We have to get permission from the public prosecutor. But given the serious nature of the crime... Armed robbery, grievous bodily harm..." He nodded. "Yes, we'll get permission. And you're right. We'll be able to use the details from the transmission towers to work out which telephone was near your daughter's all that time."

"And when you know which telephone it was," I asked, "will you be able to find the robber? And arrest him? And compare his DNA with the DNA from the balaclava? And then throw him into prison?"

"Calm down," said the detective. "It'll have to go to court first. The suspect will get a lawyer and, if he's found guilty, then the judge will decide the sentence."

"And then they'll throw the scumbag into prison!"

The detective chuckled for a second. And then he nodded firmly. "Yes, that is most definitely the plan."

SVEN

It's Saturday morning, and I've been trying to make my mind up for at least a quarter of an hour. Or more like all night.

Should I? Shouldn't I?

The way Alaska looked as a puppy—that's how I feel now. New. Strange. Like I don't know my own paws.

Like I want to bark a Christmas song.

Finally, I just do it. I call Parker.

"Hey," says Balaclava Girl's voice on the other end of the line.

"It's me," I say.

She doesn't reply.

"Sven, I mean."

"Duh, I know that! Is your back still wet?"

"What? My back?"

This conversation is not going at all as planned. All I really want to do is hang up.

"Yesterday when..." She stops. "Never mind. It doesn't matter."

I can tell from her voice that she thinks this is as weird as I do. Why didn't I just send her a text message? Calling some-one—that's what you do with your grandma.

But if I suddenly hang up now, she really will be baffled.

"Those videos..." I clear my throat. "I know it was your idea to start sending them around. That one with Benjamin is hilarious."

She laughs. "That colander on his head! And the pretty little pieces of cake."

"Yeah," I say.

Alaska's lying on the sofa beside me. Her head against my thigh, her legs stretched out.

"And?" asks Parker. "Are you coming back to school?"

I can hear it in her voice. She hopes I'm coming back.

There's a rushing sound inside my head, but Alaska is just lying there, perfectly calm. So I'm not having a seizure.

This is normal. This is just an ordinary kind of short circuit.

"Yeah, the videos are hilarious," I say. "But don't forget that Benjamin can take off his colander. You can stop barking. I *live* on Mars—remember?"

"But now Alaska lives there too! She can predict your seizures. She can warn you before you're in trouble, can't she?"

"Yeah, when I'm doing homework. Or crossing the road. But I'm talking about school. The beast doesn't go to school."

Parker's quiet for a moment.

"Why not? Why don't you just take her with you?" she asks. "To school, I mean."

The rushing inside my head is deafening now.

I look at Alaska again. With her eyes closed, she puts her front paws up beside her nose. As if she's happy about something.

"Sven!" yells Parker. Her voice doesn't sound like Balaclava Girl's now. Balaclava Girl's voice never sounded as if it had bubbles in it. "That's it—Alaska has to come to school! All day, I mean. Then she can always warn you."

"Like they'd ever agree to that," I say. "Can you imagine that happening? A dog in class? A dog walking from classroom to classroom between classes?"

"But she's an *assistance dog*. She's allowed into stores and restaurants and planes, isn't she? At school she'd obviously wear her vest. She'd be at work, just like the teachers. Teachers are allowed to go into all of the classrooms, right? And teachers are allowed to walk down the halls, aren't they?"

I don't say anything.

No way am I going to think about this. I've had enough disappointments. Yet another lot of pills that doesn't work. An operation that gets canceled. An EEG that doesn't tell them anything at all.

*   *   *

"Or have you already asked?" Parker suddenly sounds worried. "Did the principal say that Alaska can't come to school with you?"

"No, he didn't, but..."

When the beast didn't know how to predict my seizures, I didn't need her at school. At home she pressed the alarm button, and at school there were plenty of idiots who could call the emergency number if I went crashing to the floor again.

But Parker's right. Everything's different now.

Alaska isn't there just for the alarm button. She can warn me now, before I fall. And she could do that at school too.

"I promise I won't distract her," says Parker breathlessly. "Yesterday she saw a seizure coming when I was there—so she can do it! And that night in the field she chose you. She knows that she's *your* dog. But just imagine..."

She pauses.

"Just imagine," she says quietly, "if Alaska could always come to school with you from now on. If she lay under your desk every day. In our classroom. Just *being* there."

Suddenly I can't help myself. I can picture it perfectly.

The beast walking through the halls with me, with her yellow vest on her white back. Napping under my desk while I'm doing tests and buying French baguettes and learning about the Romans.

And occasionally feeling her nose nudge my leg and hearing her whine anxiously. So that I know what's up, and I can go and lie down somewhere. Somewhere in the school, in a place without any cell phones filming away. Without any losers staring open-mouthed at Circus Sven. Without any idiots instantly calling an ambulance.

Somewhere in that enormous building, in a place with just the hairy monster and me. And maybe, if she doesn't have stuff to do, with Parker too.

PARKER

It's Monday morning, and the sun's shining. Some traffic lights are green; others are red. When I cycle past the man and his dog in the last long street, we both wave. We've never spoken to each other, but that doesn't matter. He's part of my way to school now. And I'm part of his morning walk.

I put my bike in the rack, but I don't go into school yet. I push my hands into the pockets of my sky-blue jacket and I wait.

Everything could go wrong at any moment, I know that. There are criminals everywhere and even if you put one in jail, there'll be plenty of them left. I still don't get how people can live peacefully without an alarm button within reach.

But last night I suddenly thought: *OK*. So all kinds of things could go wrong at any moment. You never know what's going to happen to you. You could get shot, you could freeze and fall to the floor, you could make a fool of yourself by barking in the very first class.

But you could also find Alaska again.

You could meet Sven.

And you could discover that there are more people living on Mars than you ever imagined.

*   *   *

Finally they walk in through the gate. Sven and Alaska.

She's wearing her bright-yellow vest; his blond hair is gleaming in the sunshine. He could have a fit at any minute and in any place, but it won't take him by surprise. Alaska can warn him in time, so he won't go crashing to the floor. He doesn't bruise his hands now; the concussions are over.

Yesterday they went to visit the principal at home. Sven, his mom and dad and Alaska. To explain that she isn't an ordinary dog. Before they went, we came up with a thousand things to say to the principal. That, yes, Alaska can breathe and wag her tail and grin away with her black mouth, but that the principal should just look at her in the same way as a wheelchair. A student who can't walk is allowed to go around school in a wheelchair. Well, then Sven should be able to have his assistance dog, shouldn't he?

But the thousand things weren't needed. The principal said yes right away.

So yeah, all kinds of things could happen at any moment. You can go to a new school where you don't know anyone. And end up in a classroom with twenty-eight kids and the sweetest dog in the world.

Outside in the playground, Alaska can say hello to me by wagging her tail, but after that we ignore each other. This afternoon we're going to the woods. Then her vest can come off and she'll be off duty. But for now she's wearing her uniform, and she's at work.

Sven and I look at each other. He brushes a strand of hair off his forehead, and I put my hands back in my pockets. All over the planet, traffic lights turn red. And then green again.

"Um..." he says. "Have we ever actually spoken to each other at school? In the light? Without a helmet and a balaclava?"

I think about it. And then I nod.

"That very first day, in the entrance hall. When you walked past me and hummed 'Jingle Bells'."

"Oh yes." He looks at the ground, and then back at me. "Do you miss your balaclava?"

"No. Do you miss your helmet?"

We start laughing at the same time. And then we head inside. The three of us. Alaska walks between us. I feel brave enough for anything, and I know Sven feels the same. As we enter the black-and-white entrance hall, the giants stop yelling.

"Look at that," I whisper. "They know us. The whole school knows who we are."

Sven grins. "So what next? Are we going to save the world?"

"We've got French first," I say. "But who knows? Maybe after that."

READING GUIDE:

QUESTIONS FOR DISCUSSION

In *Talking to Alaska*, Anna Woltz explores themes of identity, invisible disability, and the battle between appearance and reality. The questions below are designed to help you explore these key ideas.

1. Sven and Parker become friends while Parker is disguised in a balaclava. Is Parker's mask necessary for their friendship to form? Do they relate to one another differently while Parker's identity is a secret?

2. How does Sven's character develop over the course of the narrative?

3. "Alaska looks back at me, and I know that she doesn't see a vague blob. She doesn't see an alien, or my illness. She sees *me*." Do you think Alaska understands Sven?

4. Is there a difference between what the characters say and what they feel? If so, why could this be?

5. What does *Talking to Alaska* teach us about disabilities? And what do you understand by the term "invisible disability"?

6. "Even if every teacher makes every class delete every video, it will still exist. Some people have already sent it to their friends at other schools. That's just how it works—that's the world." How does living in a world where nothing can ever really be deleted affect the way we behave? Is social media a force for good or bad?

7. Do you think assistance dogs should be allowed in schools?

8. Why does Parker decide to release a video of herself barking "Jingle Bells"? Is she no longer afraid of what people will think?

9. Identity is one of the book's major themes. In what ways is Parker's identity influenced by her relationship to her family? Are friends also an important part of our identity?

10. At the end of the novel, do you think Sven and Parker are more united by their similarities or their differences?

© Carli Hermès

Anna Woltz is an internationally bestselling children's author based in the Netherlands. She has written twenty-four books for young readers, which have been translated into twenty-one languages and won numerous prizes. *Talking to Alaska* won the Zilveren Griffel, one of the most prestigious literary prizes for Dutch children's books.

Laura Watkinson is an award-winning literary translator with a strong interest in children's stories. She lives in a tall, thin house on a canal in Amsterdam with her husband, two cats, and lots and lots of books.

ROCK THE BOAT

A *GOOD DAY* FOR CLIMBING TREES

by Jaco Jacobs

**Sometimes, in the blink of an eye, you do something that changes your life forever.
Like climbing a tree with a girl you don't know.**

"An inspiring story, and a really
funny one too."
Spectator, A Book of the Year

"The perfect feel-good book from one of
South Africa's top children's authors."
Amanda Craig, *New Statesman*

ROCK THE BOAT

A GOOD NIGHT FOR SHOOTING ZOMBIES

by Jaco Jacobs

Martin's life feels dull and lonely ever since his dad died.
But one day he meets Vusi, the boy next door, who
dreams of making a zombie movie. The two are plunged
head first into a wild adventure, pulling everyone they
know along with them.

"A Good Night for Shooting Zombies strikes
a perfect balance of humor and heartbreak and
helps to define what friendship really means."
Foreword, starred review

"A wonderful and exciting story with
true emotional depth."
Ross Welford, author of *Time
Travelling with a Hamster*